CASSIE'S WAR

by
ALLAN M. WINKLER

Royal Fireworks Press
Unionville, New York
Toronto, Ontario

For Jenny

Royal Fireworks Press
First Avenue
Unionville, NY 10988
(914) 726-3333
FAX: (914) 726-3824

Royal Fireworks Press
78 Biddeford Avenue
Downsview, Ontario
M3H 1K4 Canada
FAX: (416) 633-3010

ISBN: 0-88092-106-4 Paperback
        0-88092-107-2 Library Binding

Printed in the United States of America by the Royal Fireworks Printing
Company of Unionville, New York.

CHAPTER 1

Pearl Harbor

Cassie heard a strange voice as she followed Miko through the door. It was noon, and her stomach was growling, but as she entered Miko's kitchen, she knew something was wrong.

Cassie was a bit taller than Miko. Her blonde hair, pulled back in long braids, made the freckles on her face stand out. A small scar on her forehead was barely visible behind her bangs. Plaid ribbons on the braids matched her skirt. Miko, more slender, had short, dark hair. A headband kept it out of her eyes.

Looking around, Cassie saw Miko's mother, father, and brother huddled around the kitchen table.

"Is lunch ready?" Miko asked.

Mrs. Yashimoto put her finger to her lips. "Soon," she said, as her eyes returned to the radio on the table. It wasn't playing music. Just news.

"What's going on?" Cassie spoke this time.

Mr. Yashimoto looked up from his coffee cup. "War's coming" was all he said.

The announcer told the rest. Ships sunk, planes bombed, men killed—all this at Pearl Harbor. Cassie had never heard of Pearl Harbor.

"What's it mean?" Cassie asked.

"Be still," Miko's brother Kenshi snapped.

"It's all right," Mrs. Yashimoto finally said softly in her funny English. Earlier, when she had first met Miko, Cassie had trouble understanding her mother, but now it was easier. Today, she was barely conscious of an accent as Mrs. Yashimoto continued, "Japan just attacked the United States in Hawaii. It probably means war."

Cassie was still confused. "So? I know you're Japanese and all, but you've lived here for years. And Miko was born here. And she's been my friend as long as we've been in California."

"That's true," Mr. Yashimoto nodded. "But it's still bad. Lots of people have hated us for a long time. Your father for one. Now it's going to be worse."

At the mention of her father Cassie understood. Something was happening and it meant trouble for them all.

"Eat," Mrs. Yashimoto said when she finally put lunch on the table.

Rice again, Cassie thought to herself. Yuk. But she was hungry enough to eat anything.

"Eat quickly, then go home," Mrs. Yashimoto went on. "Your father and mother will be worried, and you'd better go."

"Please, Mother, can't we play," Miko pleaded. But her mother's glance told her that the matter was closed.

"Come on," Miko said. "I'll walk you part way home."

"You don't have to," Cassie answered. At nine, she knew her way around, and liked coming back and forth on her own. Secretly, though, she was grateful for the company. And she was upset at what was going on.

Together the two girls wandered away from the house. Cassie loved the Yashimoto farm, especially the red barn with its black-shingled roof. She liked to skip down the hill in front of the barn, or sometimes roll all the way to the gray wood fence that surrounded the fields of the farm. She wished she could stay here longer today.

As they left the barnyard, Cassie had a thoughtful look on her face. Her blue eyes darted back and forth as she walked through the tall grass. Miko, following a few paces behind, seemed sad to her, as if she had just been scolded by a teacher.

"What's going on?" Cassie spoke first, but got no response. She tried again. "What can I do?"

Miko remained silent. After a moment she answered.

2

"My parents are scared. They've been scared for a long time. Japan's been in the news every day. Fighting. They're worried about my grandparents, too, back there. I've never been to Japan, but to them it's still home. War means trouble."

Cassie watched a tear trickle down Miko's cheek. It frightened her. She wanted to say something.

"Maybe it's not as bad as all that," she said.

"I don't think so." Miko's voice cracked. "My father's been hearing ugly stuff when he goes to market. Some people won't buy from him anymore. They claim he's cheating them. It's not true. I know it's not true. But it still bothers him. He says it's because war's coming."

"What does that have to do with you, or me?" Cassie was still puzzled.

"I don't know," Miko answered. "But something's wrong, and I'm scared. My father says in war all kinds of people get hurt."

As Miko began to sob, Cassie put her arms around her and held her for a moment.

"Go on back," she said gently. "I'll be all right from here on. I'll see you in school tomorrow." And she headed for the shabby gray apartment that had become home.

At first, Cassie wanted to dismiss the radio reports. Pearl Harbor—she didn't even know where it was, and she didn't care. But Miko's family had jolted her. And Miko's tears made her worry even more.

As she headed toward the housing project where families from the factories lived, she wondered what her father would say. He often scared her. In the year since her family had come from Tennessee, he had grumbled constantly about the people who lived nearby. She wished he would stop complaining about the neighbors, but he seemed to dislike most of them.

"Hey, hillbilly, whereya going?" The shrill call broke the silence and jolted Cassie. She had grown used to the taunts but still hated them. They made her feel different, no matter how much she tried to ignore them. Usually she said nothing. Today she lashed back.

"Lay off, OK?"

"Hillbilly can't take it, huh?" The older boy was quick to respond. "White trash don't like it here? Go back home. My old man says your kind don't belong here anyhow."

Cassie found herself surrounded by other children, mostly younger.

"I said lay off," Cassie yelled at the older boy as she tried to ignore the rest. He just laughed as he came closer.

"My pa says you folks should get out."

Cassie had been through this before. Usually she was all right. But each time she still wished they had never come here.

"Get away," she screamed. "Get away. Leave me alone." And she began to run as fast as she could.

Faster and faster she went. She turned corners, jumped over hedges, ran through streets. It was as if she was running through the meadows and fields of the Smoky Mountains. The dingy buildings, with peeling paint and no front yards, were a far cry from the trees and streams she remembered.

At last she managed to get away. As she looked back, there was no one in sight, but she was lost. In her mad dash to escape she had strayed into a part of the project she didn't know. One street looked like all the others. Row after row of the flat, two-family apartments stretched out in front of her, each with small porch and stairs like all the rest.

Earlier Miko had broken down. Now it was Cassie's turn.

Why are we here? she thought, as big tears rolled down her cheeks. Why did Pa make us come?

Cassie knew the answers. She knew all about hard times. She remembered meals without much food, dinner conversations about being in debt, and her own fears that they would have to move. And then the long hot trip to California, so that her father could find work in the defense plants.

Cassie wasn't happy about the move. Even more than her mother and father, she had loved their farm, even if they didn't own it. She had hoped to stay there forever. She could still feel the damp earth squishing through her toes, or the tall weeds brushing against her legs as she wandered in the fields. Even when they prickled, they made her feel part of the land. Back there, the air was clean, the grass was green, and it was home. Here, near Los Angeles, the factories belched smoke night and day. Here their apartment would never be home.

Taking a breath, Cassie tried to figure out how to find her family's apartment. Wandering down first one street, then another, she finally saw the old gray Ford with the bent running board on the side her father had bought when they had arrived. She went up the porch stairs.

"About time you came home." Her father spoke sharply. "Country's goin' to war, and she's off playing with the Japs. I won't have it, Nellie."

"Relax, Adam. You said you'd let her be."

"No more," her father said. "Things are different now. Jap attack changes everything."

Cassie knew she should keep quiet. She hated it when he got like this. When her father got going, anything she said irritated him, and it was better if she just let him say what he had to say. Usually she could manage, but this time she couldn't keep quiet.

"Stop!" Cassie cried. "Miko didn't do anything. Her parents didn't do anything. Don't blame them."

"I'm sayin' that you're goin' to have to find some new friends. No more hangin' out with them Japs."

Cassie knew she should stop, but she couldn't. As tears came to her eyes again, her words came out in a flood.

"I don't care what you say," she sobbed. "Miko's my friend, and I won't leave her be. I hate the other kids in the school, and she's the only one I like."

Her father looked at Cassie, angrier, she thought, than she had ever seen him before. Her mother pushed him away and pulled Cassie to her.

"All right, love," she said. "All right. It's going to be OK."

But her father wasn't done. "She's not going back to that Yamashito family, and that's that. No child of mine's goin' to play with the Japs."

Cassie cried harder, barely able to speak. Gasping, she had to stop to catch her breath. Finally the words came. "You don't care about me. You don't care about anybody here. You don't like the neighbors. The only thing you care about is making money in the plant."

Her father paused, as if surprised she was talking back. For a moment Cassie thought he was going to back off. Please, she thought, let him leave me alone. But he wasn't done.

"You better believe it, Miss," her father growled. "I'll make money, and I'll pick our friends here. And I'll stay away from Kikes and Wops and Japs, and you will too."

Once she started, Cassie kept going. "The kids in school are just like you," she cried. "They call each other names. They laugh at me, and laugh at you. Miko's the only one who's nice to me, and you won't even let her come over. At least Ma lets me go play at her house."

"That's the end of it, hear? No more," her father yelled, his voice louder than before. "You ain't goin' there no more. And if I hear you've been over there, you'll be sorry."

Cassie couldn't contain herself.

"No," she screamed. "You can't keep me away. I'll go anyway." And she ran from the house.

As she tore down the porch, two steps at a time, she stumbled on a broken stair, then caught herself. Tears filled her eyes, and she couldn't see. She didn't know where she was headed, but she had to go.

She didn't see the battered pickup truck barreling down the road a block away.

The brakes squealed and Cassie screamed. As the truck swerved, it skidded on the pavement and brushed against the curb. Cassie was swept from her feet. Knocked down and dragged for a few yards, she lay motionless in the street.

CHAPTER 2

Hospital

Cassie lay quietly in the metal bed. She felt groggy, and a dull pain shot through her left leg.

Where am I? she wondered as she opened her eyes. What's going on?

Without turning her head, she saw that she was in a room containing other beds. Two rows of beds were crowded together, with a narrow corridor running down the middle.

It must be a hospital, she thought. She had never seen one before—she'd been born at home in Tennessee and had never been really sick—but from books she knew what hospitals were supposed to look like. This one was painted a pale green—just like the school halls—with a dull yellow floor. Tiles were broken, sometimes replaced with new ones a slightly different color. They looked dirty.

There were too many people in the room. To Cassie it looked big enough for five or six patients. Twice that many were crowded in now. Visitors gathered around the other beds. They talked and laughed with the people they had come to see.

Only Cassie was alone.

"There she is, Nellie." Cassie heard a familiar voice coming through the door to the left. She tried to turn but found it hard to move. Her leg was in a heavy cast connected to cables above the bed, and it kept her from rolling over or sitting up.

The footsteps came closer. Nellie, wiry and just a little taller than Cassie, was the first to the bed. "Cassie, Cassie." Her mother's voice cracked as she embraced her daughter in the bed.

Cassie clung to her mother then drew back and gazed at her face. She looked for a long time at her hair, pulled back into a tight bun. Her eyes wandered along her mother's forehead and cheeks as she remembered how she had always liked to look at her face. Without taking her eyes from her mother, Cassie whispered, "Ma, Why am I here?"

"You don't remember?"

"No."

"It's all right, pumpkin, it's all right."

"But why am I here?" Cassie persisted.

Stroking her head as he came closer to the bed, her father pushed the hair back from her eyes. "You ran into a truck," he answered.

Still Cassie was puzzled. She looked up at her father and noticed the lines on his face. He had on a short-sleeved shirt, and she could see the muscles in his arms. His hand felt good; he seldom held her head that way, but she liked it when he did. She wished he would do it more often. Now she was torn between finding out more and just enjoying her father's touch.

She rested quietly for a while. Despite the pain in her leg, the presence of her parents helped. Vaguely sick to her stomach, she felt better with them here.

Finally she spoke again. "What truck? What happened?"

"Fellow ran you over," her father said. "Come tearing down the street and near wiped you out. I'd like to get the guy who did it."

"Please, Adam. Let it be." Cassie cringed as her parents began to talk above her head. "It's over now."

"It's not over. Look at her, strapped to them wires."

"Please, Adam." Cassie thought her mother sounded more insistent now, just like when she got peeved at her. "I don't want to talk about it now."

"Have it your way. You'll see."

Cassie watched her mother whirl around. "If you hadn't been so pig-headed when she came back from Miko's, this wouldn't have happened. It's as much your fault as his."

"Oh no you don't," her father answered. "Whose side you on, anyhow?"

"No sides, Adam. All I'm saying is it's bad enough having Cassie here, and I wish we hadn't gotten her upset enough to go running in the street."

Her father shrugged, rubbing her head again. "Well, kiddo, what goes?"

Cassie pulled Nellie closer, as if that would make it easier to respond. She wished again that her parents would just hold her and stop arguing. It was bad enough at home. Here in the hospital it was even worse. She wanted to hold them both. She didn't want to say anything. For a long time she remained silent, until she realized that her father was waiting for her to respond. But what could she say?

Sobbing softly, Cassie started to speak. She knew she should be careful, but went ahead anyway. They couldn't hurt her here, she figured. "You never liked Miko and you kept her away. But she's my friend, and she's the only one who's nice here. I like her. And her family, and their farm."

"Just like your mother." Her father interrupted her.

"And you never listen to me either." As soon as she spoke, Cassie wished she hadn't. She wanted to say lots of things—how she wished they hadn't left Tennessee, how she dreamed of going back home. But that wouldn't help, and she knew it. With eyes closed, Cassie heard her father take a deep breath.

"I hear you, Cass, and I'm sorry, but things are different now. War's coming with the Japs. Maybe I was wrong before, but now you'd better realize we're on different sides. They're not like you, and you'd best stay away."

Cassie tried to protest, then stopped. She felt herself fading into the background like she did whenever they fought. Why couldn't her father just put his arms around her now, like he did when she was smaller? Why couldn't he hug her, with his stubbly face close to hers, so it scratched but still made her feel he cared. She loved him. She liked it when he fixed broken toys, or brought her candy on the weekends. She especially liked it when he took her wandering through the department stores, even when they didn't buy

10

anything. But why did he sometimes make it so hard? Tears came to her eyes again as she squeezed her mother's hand.

A door opened at the end of the hall. Two doctors in white coats entered the ward and walked toward Cassie's bed. One looked younger than the other, the black plastic tube on his stethoscope the color of his hair. The older one had a wide tie with funny shapes on it, just like the ties Mr. Schmitt, the principal at her school, wore. Both doctors scared her. The only time she had seen a doctor before was to get a tetanus shot when she stepped on a rusty nail back in Tennessee, and that had hurt.

"What do you think?" The younger one spoke first.

"I'm not sure. Looks bad. Fracture, bone smashed from knee to hip."

"Think it'll heal right?"

"Don't know. Can't be sure in these cases. Traction should help. We'll just have to hope for the best."

The doctors were standing near the bed, talking to themselves as if no one else was there. Cassie watched her mother, who was becoming irritated at being ignored. Now she wished her father was still around, but he had gone home to tinker with the car he needed to take to work tomorrow.

"When can she go home?" the younger doctor asked the other.

"Week. Two weeks. We'll take pictures in a while and see how it's set."

Nellie finally could wait no longer. "Is her leg going to be all right?" she asked.

"I hope so." The older doctor turned her way. "We've done all we could, but it was pretty bad. The truck must have crushed her leg. We've got the bone in place with pins now, but its going to take some time."

Nellie took a deep breath. "What can we do?"

"Not much for a while. Keep her amused here. Keep her quiet when you take her home."

"When's that?"

11

"Like I said, a week or two."

The doctor sounded impatient to Cassie, as if he was eager to leave. She wanted him to go, so she could talk to her mother again. But she also wanted to find out what was going on. Overwhelmed by the doctors in their white coats, she was too scared to say anything.

Her mother took charge. "When we get her home, what should we do?"

"Keep her off her leg. We'll get you some crutches. She'll be on them for a couple of months."

"And then?"

"Hope for the best."

Cassie thought Nellie sounded frustrated by the doctor's remark. She went on. "When will we know how well she can walk again?"

As she heard her mother ask her questions, Cassie felt even more frightened than before. She thought of climbing trees back home, then of running down the hill by Miko's barn, and suddenly realized that she might not be able to do that again, at least not for a while.

The doctor's response wasn't reassuring. "We won't know much for sure until the cast's off and we can check the bone."

"She's got to walk right, you hear." Nellie sounded desperate.

"We'll do the best we can." The doctors looked as though they were in a hurry to move on. "We'll check on her tomorrow, and let you know where things stand then."

As the doctors left the ward, another man came through the door. Darker-skinned, with black hair, Cassie thought he looked Mexican. At least he looked a little like the few Mexican kids she'd seen in school. Cassie didn't know him, and didn't think her mother did either, for she looked up, then turned back to her.

The man stood at the far end of the room and gazed around. His eyes moved from one bed to the next and he seemed to be looking for someone.

He stared at Cassie's bed. Then slowly, awkwardly, he moved toward her.

"Excuse me. You must be girl I hit with my truck." He spoke quietly with an accent, though not as strong as Miko's mother's.

Cassie heard her mother gasp.

"Excuse me," he repeated. "I'm not sure what to say. I just wanted you to know I'm sorry." He paused, glancing over at Cassie, then looking away, as if embarrassed to catch her eye. Cassie saw him look over at her mother as he continued, "You don't want to see me, but I had to come. I know what you're feeling. I have a daughter too. I can't get your girl out of my mind."

Cassie closed her eyes.

"My name's Garcia, Manuel Garcia." There was a long pause. "I never saw her till it was too late. When she darted out, I couldn't stop."

Cassie felt funny as she listened to people talk about her as if she wasn't there.

"I want to help. I don't make much, but I want to do whatever I can."

Cassie opened her eyes and looked over at the man. She noticed dark lines under his eyes when he seemed to squint. He's hurting too, she thought. She smiled at him and reached out as he held out his hand.

As the man apologized once more, Cassie heard her father whistle as he came through the door. That was a good sign, she thought. Maybe he wouldn't be mad any more. Ever. She watched her father as he saw the stranger by her bed. She could tell as he stiffened that he didn't like the light-brown man who was neither a doctor nor a member of the hospital staff.

"What do you want?" There was a nasty edge to his voice.

"I came to apologize for the accident today."

"So?" Cassie watched her father's face as he realized who the man was. "Why don't you just go back where you belong."

Cassie cringed. Her father was talking just like he did at home whenever he got angry at any of the neighbors. Usually, though, they couldn't hear. This time the man had to deal with her father's frustration. She watched him pause.

"I am sorry for what happened earlier," he said softly.

"Thank the Lord." Her father sounded brusque, as he often was to her when he wasn't happy with her explanation for why she'd done something.

The man looked at her father, then looked down.

"Just git out and don't come back." Her father ignored any sympathy he may have had for the other man and let his anger surface. He paused for a moment, but when the Mexican made no move, he went on, nastier all the time. "You've done enough damage already. You'd better get outa here quick as you can before I move you along."

The man kept his composure and remained still.

"Just git."

Cassie tried to roll over, then turned her head. She hadn't minded the visitor. She wanted her father here, but not this way. It made her feel even worse to watch him lose his temper.

"Please, Adam." Cassie's mother spoke from near the head of the bed.

"Quiet!" Cassie's father whirled around to face her.

"Hear him out. It wasn't his fault."

"I don't care!"

In the back of the room Cassie began to cry. "Ma, Ma, make Pa stop." But her plea fell on deaf ears. Through her tears, she could see her father's cheeks redden, like they did when he was really angry.

Slowly, the man turned and left.

With only her parents by her bed, Cassie continued to sob. Her leg hurt more now, as if the crying made it throb. She wanted to say something to her mother and father, but she didn't know what to say.

"I want to go home." It was all she could get out. It could have meant anything. Even Cassie wasn't sure what she meant.

14

Her father looked puzzled as he sat down next to her. He took Cassie's hand, while her mother quietly stroked her head. Cassie felt relieved that the episode was over. In a few minutes her sobs ceased, and at least for the moment the hurt began to fade.

It was evening now, and time for her parents to go. Cassie wanted them to stay, but there was nothing she could do. She wanted to talk, but no words came. Nellie and Adam both kissed her good night. As she lay back on the bed and watched them leave, she was aware of a lump forming in her throat. Cassie felt all alone.

CHAPTER 3

School

Cassie hobbled into the kitchen. "I'd better hurry," she said as she sat down at the table and picked up her juice. "I don't want to be late for school."

"Eat your breakfast first," Nellie answered. "You'll make it if you're quick."

Cassie smiled. "You always say that," she said. "And I was late last week." And she began to eat her oatmeal while drinking her juice at the same time.

Cassie had been home for a month and was finally feeling better. The weeks in the hospital had been especially hard. She was grateful that her parents had come every day. She needed them and had been relieved that after the first day, they hadn't argued much in front of her. At first, she could remember just laying quietly in traction, with her leg extended by the cables over the bed. Then the doctors had let her move around a bit. But all she wanted to do was come home.

Back in the apartment, she could feel things start to return to normal. Her leg stopped hurting. More than before, her father brought her things on the way home from work, a doll with a porcelain face one time, a puzzle of the California coast another. But he still seemed edgy, abrupt with both her and her mother. He was working a lot, she knew, more than back in Tennessee, and it made him tired all the time. And her mother seemed more moody now, retreating into long silences when she seemed lost in her own thoughts.

Cassie hadn't thought much earlier about whether her mother liked it here, but now she realized how much both of them wanted to go home.

Putting down her spoon, Cassie got up and hopped toward the door, both crutches in her left hand. "Bye, Ma," she called as she took one porch stair at a time, holding on to the rail. "I'll be back at noon."

Rounding the corner, Cassie saw Miko up ahead. Her father had forbidden her to go back to Miko's house, but he had said nothing about walking to school. So Cassie had taken to meeting Miko each morning once she was safely around the corner from the apartment. Her father was at the factory and wouldn't know. And her mother probably knew what she was doing but wouldn't say anything.

Her cast had become a nuisance, but she was getting used to the crutches and had no trouble getting around. She moved faster to catch up.

Miko's face lit up. "Hi, Cassie."

The two girls walked together silently for a moment. Then Miko began hopping in imitation of Cassie's awkward gait.

"What're you doing?" Cassie asked.

"Walking, silly," Miko said.

"So, walk right."

"I am."

Cassie smiled and fell into the game they sometimes played. She began to hobble faster, using her crutches as effectively as she could. She had three legs to Miko's two but was still slower on her feet.

"All right already. You win." Cassie stopped as she conceded defeat. Breathless, both girls paused for a moment before starting again for school.

"What's the matter?" Cassie asked after they had walked together without speaking for a while. Miko had been gay a few moments ago when they first met. Now she had a frown on her face.

"Nothing," Miko answered as she kicked a stone in the street.

"Come on. Something's bothering you. Is it still my father?"

"It's not him. It's my own parents."

"What about them?"

"They're worried about what's happening. The war's scaring them. My father had to go downtown, and they asked him all kinds of funny questions in some office. And people won't buy his fruits

17

or vegetables anymore. Just yesterday, someone threw a rock at his stall in the market."

Cassie nodded. "I saw the papers the other day," she said. "It's spooky. My father read aloud a section about 'yellow vermin' and said the Japs realized they weren't welcome here. I started to say something, but he just got mad."

"That's not all," Miko responded. "I read that too, but there's more. My parents are hearing rumors about having to leave here. I don't know where we could move to. I'm scared. I don't want to go."

"Go where?"

"Who knows. We don't know anyone outside of here. I don't know what we'll do.

"It's OK." Cassie tried to comfort her friend. "Maybe the war'll be over soon, we won't have to worry." Even as she spoke though, she knew that things weren't going to get better for some time.

As the girls neared the school, Cassie began to think about things Miss Daniel had said their fifth grade class would be doing.

"Valentine's Day's coming up," she said. "Will you be mine?"

"Only if you'll be mine."

"What'll you give me?"

"Wait and see."

Turning into the playground, they steered clear of the other children and walked toward the door. Boys were running in every direction, chasing one another in the few moments before school began. Cassie had never much liked the rough play before. Now, with her cast, she was even more scared of being knocked down.

"Let's go in and see if Miss Daniel will let us make valentines."

Miko nodded, and the two girls went into the school.

The bell jangled and the rest of the fifth grade class filed in. Sam, one of the larger bullies in the class, deliberately stumbled over Cassie's crutch and then got mad. Cassie just ignored him.

The room was crowded. There were forty kids in the class, and that was just in the morning. Another forty came in the afternoon.

"Good morning, class."

"Good morning, Miss Daniel."

That ritual completed, Miss Daniel looked up and down the rows to see who was absent. Cassie watched her intently. She liked the first few moments of the school day, when everthing seemed in place.

She also liked looking at Miss Daniel. She was the first young teacher Cassie had ever had. Thin, with shoulder-length blonde hair, she usually seemed eager and lively, and Cassie liked to imagine herself in Miss Daniel's place. Today, though, she seemed tired. Some of the boys had been giving her a hard time, Cassie remembered, and it disrupted class for everyone.

"What're we going to do today?" Sam whined from the back of the room. "Not valentines?"

"Oh, yes, Miss Daniel. You promised," a girl near the front chimed in.

"I ain't gonna do no valentines," Sam's friend, equally large, said.

Looking behind her, Cassie stared at the troublemakers. She knew she should keep quiet but felt safe in the classroom and comfortable speaking up. "Some of us happen to like Valentine's Day, Sam. Why don't you just let us be."

"Who's gonna give you a valentine, hillbilly?"

"That's enough." Miss Daniel's voice broke in before Cassie had a chance to respond.

"I ain't giving her no valentine," Sam continued. "And I sure ain't giving one to her Jap friend."

The class was still for a moment. Miko was the only Japanese-American child in the class. Cassie had been hearing whispers about her for the past few weeks and hoped that Miko hadn't heard them herself. But this was the first time anything direct had been said that couldn't be ignored.

"I said that's enough." Miss Daniel tried to regain control, without success.

19

"What're the Japs doing in our school anyway?" Sam refused to let the matter drop. "My Pa says we oughta throw the whole lot of 'em out. Send 'em back to Japan."

"My pa too."

"And mine." Other students joined in the attack.

Cassie glanced over at Miko. She remained quiet, but her face had grown pale. She was squinting, as if to hold back tears, and her nose looked scrunched up. Cassie wanted to do something for her but didn't know what to do. She was also glad that this attack hadn't focused on her.

"That's enough!" Miss Daniel's voice rose, and her tone became hard. "Sam, I don't want to hear that kind of talk again. You listen to me for a moment. You and I both know there's a war on, and we're fighting the Japanese. But Miko's done nothing to you, and she has as much right to be here as you. Why, your relatives came from elsewhere some time ago, too."

"I don't know about that, ma'am. We been here as long as I can remember."

The other kids laughed. Miss Daniel looked uncomfortable but was determined to remain in charge. "You heard me, Sam. Miko's done nothing to you. You leave her alone. I hear that nasty talk again, and you'll have to leave at once."

"Okay by me." Sam continued in the same insolent tone. "I'd just as soon go someplace where we's all real Americans."

"Last warning, Sam."

The boy was still.

Cassie was still upset later in the day. She couldn't help feeling an undercurrent of unrest in the classroom. Miss Daniel seemed tense and snapped at noisy kids more than usual. And Miko looked glum. Cassie could tell she was struggling to seem impassive, but was having a hard time. Every so often her bottom lip quivered like it did when she was really disturbed.

The Valentine's Day party before dismissal helped brighten things up for a while. Cassie had made valentines for all of the girls and for a few of the boys she let herself like. She picked out a special one, but not too big, for one of the nicer boys she sometimes talked to named Joel.

"One for you, and one for you, and one for you." She and the others went around the room, handing the cards to their friends.

As she got to the back of the class, she suddenly realized that she had forgotten a valentine for Maria, the new Mexican girl in the back row. Maria sat by herself, not really part of any group yet. Others had forgotten her as well.

How long had she been here? Cassie tried to remember. Maria had first come to the school during the month she'd been in the hospital. They hadn't said much to each other since she'd been back. In fact, Maria hadn't said much to anybody in that time. Every once in a while, Sam and some of the others had made nasty cracks about wetbacks, but that was nothing new. Preoccupied with her own problems and with Miko's, Cassie simply hadn't paid much attention to the new girl in the back.

I've got to do something, Cassie thought to herself.

"Do you have a valentine for Maria," she whispered to Miko as she turned to return to her own seat.

Miko shook her head.

"Do you have an extra one?"

Again Miko shook her head.

Cassie had one left, the one she had intended for Miko. Torn as she tried to decide what to do, she finally erased the name on it, and wrote Maria on the envelope instead. Miko would understand, she thought. I'll make her something special after school.

Taking the card to the back of the room, she found Maria staring at her. Cassie dropped the valentine on the desk. Maria just continued to stare.

After noon dismissal, Cassie stayed in the classroom for a few moments to cut and paste a special valentine for Miko. Miko watered plants, washed the blackboard and picked up the chalk as she waited for Cassie to walk home.

Finishing up the special card, Cassie handed it to Miko. "You know why it's late, don't you?"

Miko nodded. "That was nice of you. I saw what you did. I don't mind."

"This one's more special, anyway," Cassie said. On the card she had written "To my best friend, always," with lots of XXXXs underneath.

As Cassie limped out the door with Miko by her side, she saw Maria standing near the exit. The Mexican girl came closer as Cassie and Miko passed.

"Thank you for the valentine," she said shyly.

"You're welcome."

Maria stood still, not yet ready to leave. She ran her hand through her short dark brown hair.

She looked like she was trying to say something, Cassie thought, but it wouldn't come out.

"You know who I am, don't you?" The words finally came.

Cassie shook her head.

"My father was driving the truck that...that hit you." Tears formed in her eyes, almost in relief at having gotten a long-locked secret out.

Cassie felt a tingling as Maria spoke. She didn't know what to say. She hadn't thought much about the accident, or about who had hit her. Now, with Maria's admission, memories of the accident returned.

She looked at Maria for a moment. "I didn't know," she said at last.

"I'm sorry," Maria said. "I just wanted to tell you."

Unsure of what to do, Cassie smiled gently and patted Maria's arm. Maria stood very still for a moment as she looked back at Cassie, then turned and left the hallway. Cassie and Miko started home.

CHAPTER 4

Work

Cassie sat across from her mother at the kitchen table. It was a Saturday morning in March, and school was out. She dawdled with her orange juice as her mother drank a second cup of coffee and stared outside.

"What's wrong, Ma?"

Her mother continued staring out the window.

"Ma, is something bothering you? Have I done something wrong?"

"It's not you at all, pumpkin," her mother finally answered. "It's just…." and then she broke off.

Torn over whether to repeat her question or to wait for her mother to start again, Cassie remained silent. After a few moments her mother sighed.

"I know you're not happy here, Cassie," she said. "I feel out of touch too. I came because Pa wanted to come, and I thought it would be better for you. But now I wonder if we shouldn't have just stayed back home."

Cassie sat very still. Sometimes she and her mother talked like this, but it had always been about her and what she was doing. This was the first time her mother had opened up about herself.

"Did we have to come, Ma?" Cassie knew the answer even before her mother spoke.

"There was no work for your pa back in Tennessee, and the factories here were making stuff for the war. He figured he could make it if he worked in a plant, to save some money and someday buy us our own home."

"But why did we have to come?"

"No way a woman can stay back if her man wants to move. It was hard enough for the month or two when he came out ahead, and we waited so you could finish school."

Cassie had a different memory of those months. She remembered how easy it was at home. It was quieter, brighter being alone with her mother. But Cassie knew from the start that it wasn't going to last. Her mother needed her father. She loved him, Cassie guessed, even if she didn't always like some of the things he did, and depended on him. She'd been through a lot with him. And she knew she couldn't take the constant questions of the Tennessee neighbors who wondered when she was going to follow him west.

Cassie watched her mother drift for a moment as if dreaming of another time. "What's going to happen now, Ma?"

"I'm not sure. I'm just not sure." Nellie looked around at the sparely furnished apartment. They had the basic things—a couch, a kitchen table and chairs, a couple of beds—and some faded pictures of fields and rivers on the wall. But the warm things—the rugs and quilts and blankets she had made to use or hang as decorations back home—none of those was here. She couldn't carry them on the train, and so she had given them to the neighbors to save before they left. Now she missed them all the more.

Watching intently, Cassie knew that her mother hated the cold apartment with the paper-thin walls as much as she did. It irritated her to be able to hear the neighbors at all hours of the day and night, to feel constantly surrounded by people at all times. Cassie knew they couldn't change those things, but maybe they could brighten the place up. "Can't you make some more quilts and stuff like you did back home?" she asked. Her mother had been wonderful with her hands. She could crochet a bright- colored potholder in a couple of hours, a granny-square blanket in a week. But she hadn't done a thing since she had been in California.

"I don't know. I just don't seem to feel like it. I go out, I shop, I clean. But I just don't feel like working on those things like I used to. I should. I know. For you. For Pa. For me. But it's so hard."

She paused for a moment. "Lord knows, though, I've got to do something."

Cassie understood. She at least had Miko, whom she could see on school days. But her mother was isolated, cut off from the life she had known back home. Ma, more than Pa, had been rooted in Tennessee, comfortable with the life they led, however poor it had been. Before Cassie could respond, her mother began to speak again.

"Have you seen those posters down by the stores, Cassie? The ones asking women to work?"

Cassie nodded.

"Well, I've been thinking. It might be nice to get a job. That'd at least give me something to do."

Cassie scowled. The mothers of some of the kids at school worked. Joel's mother had just taken a job as a secretary. But Cassie had never known her mother to work in any outside job before.

"Sadie down the block, you know Sadie." Sadie was Nellie's only friend in the project. Transplanted too, she came from Kentucky. Her husband was a welder like Pa, making more money than ever before but seldom around. "Sadie told me she's going to work in one of the new plants," Nellie said. "They need people to work the machines, and with the war on now, and men being drafted into the army and going to fight, they need anybody there. I bet I could get a job too."

"Doing what?"

"I don't know. Working in the steel plant, maybe. Or in the shipyard. Sadie says there's jobs for the asking in the shipyard."

"What would Pa say?"

Nellie's face clouded. "I don't think he'd like it. He didn't mind me workin' in our garden back home, but he wouldn't let me work in the store when Jack needed someone to help him that time. That's what's bothering me now, I guess. I think I want to go work, but I don't know how to ask."

The conversation was cut short as Cassie's father came in the door. He had been out puttering with the car, and was covered with grease.

"Got it working, Nellie." He looked pleased with himself.

"Good. But please don't sit down here with all that gunk on you."

Ignoring the request, her father dropped into a chair and plunked his elbows on the table. "I can take you shopping now. We better use the car while we can, though. Gas rationing's coming and we won't be able to get around much, except to go to work."

"What's rationing?" Cassie asked.

"It's when you don't got much stuff, but a lot of people want it. And so they're willing to pay more for it."

"So?"

"Well, you got to do something about high prices. So rationing is when someone—usually the government—says you can only have so much of something. I guess that's what's goin' to happen now."

"There's not a whole lot of gas?" Cassie was curious now.

"That's the dang fool thing about it," her father answered. "Seems like there's lots of gas, only there ain't so much rubber for tires. And so the government thinks it can save rubber by keeping us from getting gas."

Cassie thought about that for a moment, then fell silent. She wasn't sure she understood. But there was a whole lot about the war she didn't understand.

A little later, Cassie followed her mother and father out the door. They were heading downtown. The used refrigerator they had bought when they arrived was wearing out, and they were going to look for a better one. The one good thing about living here, Cassie thought to herself, was that they could buy some new things now.

Her father whistled as they went down the steps. Cassie understood how much he looked forward to these shopping expeditions now that there was money to spend. This was his way of taking care of them and doing things for the family, she guessed. And, she had to admit to herself, she liked it, too. They had gotten a better stove a couple of weeks ago, and it was a real treat to have four working burners for the first time.

Her father's whistling turned to singing. "So long, Mama, I'm off to Yokohama," he sang quietly, under his breath, off-key. Cassie smiled at his song. Yokohama was in Japan, she knew from talking to Miko's mother a while ago, but it didn't matter. It just made her feel better when Pa was in a good mood.

And she was pleased to be getting out. Her cast had limited how much she could get around, and for a long time she had felt cooped up. She was almost mended now, she knew, for the cast had come off a week ago, and she could walk on her own. She had a limp and couldn't run or jump but figured she'd be able to do that soon enough.

Cassie coughed as she got into the car.

"You OK, girl?" her father asked.

Cassie nodded. Her throat hurt, and she knew she was getting another cold, but she didn't want to say anything for fear she would be left behind. It seemed as if she had gotten one cold after another after they had left Tennessee.

"I'm fine," she finally answered, curling up in the back seat, wishing once more that she was back home in Tennessee.

When they got back from the store, her father was in a good mood. He wandered around, tightening a few loose hinges, tacking down a loose board by the kitchen window, and making other repairs. The new used refrigerator he had just bought was a better buy than the first, and he had been able to trade the old one to reduce the cost. He liked living in Los Angeles, Cassie knew, dickering with store owners, buying things he hadn't been able to afford before.

Quietly, Cassie set the table. She thought about the trip downtown, about having to drive miles to get anywhere, and wondered what would happen when there was no more gas. Then she wondered about her mother. She had been strangely silent all afternoon, saying little as her father took charge. Was she thinking about what they had talked about earlier? Cassie thought so but wasn't sure. Cassie worried about her mother but didn't know what to do. When she was off with Miko, she could bounce out of her mood and be herself, but it was harder at home when her mother seemed preoccupied. Cassie wished her mother would have Sadie over more often. It would help if she had someone to talk to more.

Sitting down to meat loaf and mashed potatoes, the three ate in silence for a time. Finally, after finishing her meal, Cassie watched as her mother pushed her plate away, looked at Pa, and said, "Adam, I want to go to work."

Her father dropped his fork. "You what?" he said.

"You heard me. I want to go to work."

"Ain't no jobs for women."

"That's not true," Nellie answered. "There's posters all over the place advertising jobs. Sadie says they're hiring at the shipyard. They need people now the draft's taking all the men."

Cassie listened without saying a word. She had sensed that her mother was going to say something but hadn't realized it was going to come this soon.

Her father's lips tightened, and his face grew grim. His cheeks reddened. Wrinkling his forehead and frowning, he looked at her mother and said, "No woman of mine's going to work."

"Why not?"

Her father was silent for a spell. "I know some women are starting to work," he said finally. "There's a couple on my floor. But no woman of mine's goin' to work."

"Why not?" her mother persisted.

"'Cause I came up here so as to take care of you and Cassie, and we're doin' just fine."

"We're not!" Cassie stared as her mother interrupted him. She usually didn't do that, but she was angry now. "You buy what you want, what you think we need, but then pinch pennies all the rest of the time. I can't get anything I want, unless you think it's OK. Can't

28

buy this, can't buy that. Sure it's better than back home, but that's only 'cause we had nothing at all back there."

"This is home now, and you'd better not forget it." Her father looked more stubborn. He wasn't going to give an inch, Cassie knew. When he got into an argument, he was going to win it, whatever it took.

"I don't know where home is anymore," her mother went on. "But I do know I'm going out of my mind. I've got to do something."

"Why don't you knit or quilt anymore, like you used to? Be a real woman again?"

Her mother took a deep breath. "I don't feel like it, and anyway, there's no one to do it with. I'm lonesome here, Adam. I feel all alone."

Her father's face softened for a moment, then Cassie saw his mouth tighten again. This was a little like watching a puppet show, she thought, only her parents weren't puppets. And her father didn't look like he was going to budge.

"Sadie's going to work next week. Got a job already. I want to try too."

Her father just shook his head. "Nope, won't do. Sadie's got no kids. She can do what she wants. It's different for you."

"Come on. Cassie can take care of herself. She's a big girl now."

"Yeah. Look what she did to herself last December. Almost killed herself."

"That's not my fault, and you know it. And anyway, you know why she went tearing out the house." Her mother's eyes were beginning to fill with tears.

"That's neither here nor there, Nellie. Anyway, like I said, no wife of mine's going to work, and that's that."

Cassie watched her mother leave the table, go into the bedroom, and slam the door.

29

With the weekend over, Cassie was back in school. That meant she could see Miko again, but Miko seemed strange. As they played with a rubber ball on the playground, Miko didn't say much at all.

Walking home, Cassie poked Miko in the ribs, trying to tickle her. Usually it worked. Miko was really ticklish, and liked it when she got giggling and couldn't stop. Cassie wasn't quite as excitable, but played along, for she liked it too when Miko tried to get her going.

"Stop it," Miko said. "Please. I just don't feel like it right now."

"You OK?" Cassie asked.

"I don't know," Miko answered.

Just then Joel caught up with them. "I found a nickel on the playground," he said. "Want some candy at the store?"

Cassie was about to say yes, but Miko shook her head. "My mother needs me at home," she said.

Cassie wanted to go off with him. He'd smiled at her a couple of times in the last few weeks, and was one of the few boys who said hello. But all she said was "Thanks" as she followed Miko toward the farm.

As they neared her apartment and said goodbye, Cassie was surprised to see their car in front of the apartment. That's strange, she thought. Usually her father didn't come home until dinner time. Maybe he was on the early shift today. No, she remembered him leaving for work as she was getting up.

She heard voices rising as she entered the kitchen. Her parents were sitting at the table.

"I've got no choice. You know that. You knew that when you called the plant." Her father was talking.

"I know, I know. You've got to go. But what'll we do?"

Cassie looked at both of them. They became quiet as they looked back at her, each waiting for the other to speak.

"Your pa's been drafted." Nellie finally broke the silence. "He's got to go next month."

"I thought the Army'd miss me, but I guess not. You two girls'll be on your own."

Cassie's first thought was that she could now return to Tennessee.

As if reading her mind, her mother said, "We'll stay here, Cassie, you and me. We can't make it at home. Pa'll send money, but we're going to have to do something too. I'll be getting a job." Her face remained impassive, but Cassie thought she could see the satisfaction shining in her eyes. She'd won the argument. She'd have to work if the family was going to survive.

Cassie was shocked.

"Why you?" was all she could say to her father.

"Lots of men going," he answered. "Not many's going to get out."

Cassie was puzzled by her parents. They had seemed agitated when she came in but deep down didn't seem particularly concerned, she thought. Her father like to move, liked change, she thought. This was his chance to get away, and he was probably even looking forward to it. And somehow her mother didn't seem too disappointed either. This would let her get out of the house.

"There's not much we can do I suppose," she finally said.

"Nope," her father answered. "Not much at all."

Later that afternoon, Cassie walked outside by herself. She wanted to talk to her mother, but she was hovering around her father as if he was going to leave anytime. Cassie felt vaguely unsettled. Uncomfortable with her father, she was still shocked at the thought of him leaving. On the one hand, she was almost relieved; on the other hand, she didn't want him to go.

CHAPTER 5

Evacuation

Cassie left the house as quickly as she could. The past week had been particularly hard. Her father had been irritable and hard to have around. Ever since his draft notice had come, he had been thinking about the Army. He had continued to work for a while, then had quit his job to spend some time at home before shipping out. But he found it hard hanging around the house when he really wanted to leave. To Cassie he seemed more of a nuisance than ever before.

"Be home after school," he called as she closed the door behind her.

Cassie didn't respond. Looking back at the front steps, she made sure that no one was watching as she walked away. She headed up the street, skipping more easily as her leg continued to improve. Turning the corner, she met Miko at the usual spot.

"Hi," Cassie said.

Miko gave a half-smile in return, then dropped her head and concentrated on scuffling up the dirt with her feet as she walked along. She grunted as she stubbed her toe on a rock.

Cassie responded immediately to Miko's mood. "What's wrong?" she asked. "You can tell me."

Miko remained silent. Cassie could see that she was fighting back tears. She took Miko's arm, and made her pause. "What's wrong," she asked again.

"We're leaving," Miko finally said.

Cassie wasn't sure what she meant. "Where to?" she asked, puzzled. "Why?"

"My father says the Army's ordering all Japanese away from here. We have a few days to pack everything and get out."

"And leave the farm?" Cassie wondered what was going on. The Army was taking her father, but he was going to fight in the war. Why did Miko have to leave?

"Where are you going to?" she asked at last.

"They're telling us to go to some assembly center." Miko sobbed. "I don't know where it is, but my father says lots of Japanese from around here'll be there."

Cassie remembered Miko's fears a month ago. Her own father hadn't said anything about what was happening to the Japanese. Except for an occasional nasty comment about "rotten Japs" in the war, he hadn't paid much attention to what was happening to them here.

"Is your whole family going?"

Miko nodded.

"Will you come back?"

Miko shrugged her shoulders as she continued to cry.

"Your farm'll still be here. No one'll take it." Cassie tried to sound reassuring, but she too wondered what would happen after Miko's family went. "I'll be here. I'll watch it and I'll wait for you." Cassie knew she wasn't making much sense. Still, she wanted to say something.

Cassie bit her bottom lip, then paused for a few moments until Miko caught her breath. Finally they began to walk again, neither saying a word. Cassie's arm remained around Miko as they entered the school yard. The bell clanged just then, and both hurried for the door.

It was hard to concentrate in school. Cassie's mind kept coming back to what Miko had said. She really didn't understand it, and thought about asking Miss Daniel to help explain why Miko's family was being ordered to go, but then thought of Sam and the other rough boys in the back and decided it was better not to raise the issue.

Miko, too, seemed preoccupied. She answered when called upon and did all Miss Daniel asked, but Cassie could see that her thoughts were elsewhere. Sometimes she stared out the window, looking at nothing in particular, with a frown on her face.

When the morning was finally over, Cassie and Miko left school together. Occasionally they stayed after to help Miss Daniel clean blackboards and erasers, but today both wanted to leave.

They got out of the school yard as quickly as they could to avoid the kids in the afternoon session who had already started to arrive. Some boys were playing baseball in a lot near the school. The two girls hurried past, hoping that they would be left alone.

"I'm coming over," Cassie said as they walked along the street bordering the school.

"You can't do that. Your father'll get mad."

"I don't care. He's leaving soon, and he won't know. Anyway, what can he do to me now?"

Miko was still worried. "Are you sure you'll be OK? I mean, my mother'd be really glad to see you. But I'd feel bad if you got in trouble for coming."

"Don't worry about me," Cassie said. "I'll be all right."

It felt wonderful wandering through the fields toward the farm again. Cassie hadn't been along this route since the accident. For a long time she had been on crutches, and had to stay on flat surfaces. And since she had been forbidden to go to Miko's, she had stayed away from the fields altogether. Now she could feel the grass rustling around her legs as they walked along. She loved hearing the sound of the California quail in the trees. She hadn't realized how much she had missed the farm.

Cassie knew that Miko was still upset but found herself feeling better than before. She couldn't help it. She just breathed deeply and walked contentedly toward the house.

As they entered the front door, Mrs. Yashimoto looked up from the box she was packing. She saw Cassie, and her face lit up. She got up and went over to her, hugged her and held her tight. Cassie was surprised. Usually Miko's mother was reserved. She was nice, but she always tried to keep her feelings to herself.

"Cassie, Cassie."

"Hello, Mrs. Yashimoto."

"Goodness, look at you. You look just like when we saw you last. My, it's good to see you again." Her accent was just as Cassie remembered it. Her eyes took Cassie in from head to toe, stopping at the long purple scar on her leg.

Cassie felt her glance but didn't care. "It's OK," she said. "It's all healed now, and I'm not limping much anymore."

"I know, I know. Miko's told me. But I need a chance to see for myself."

"What're you doing here?" Cassie looked at the boxes strewn around the room, and at the piles of books and papers and clothes. She wasn't sure how much she should ask, but she wanted to know.

"I'm trying to pack everything up in the next few days before we have to leave. We've been here for years. Now we've got to go through all that we own, to see what we can sell, and what we can store until we return."

"Where are you putting things?" Cassie asked.

"A few of the neighbors will take some of the bigger pieces of furniture and valuables. Most of the other things Miko's father is taking to the second-hand stores to sell for what he can."

"That won't be too bad, will it?" Cassie asked.

Mrs. Yashimoto shook her head sadly. "We won't get much. Everybody's trying to sell right now, and the dealers can set the price. But that's not the worst of it. I can't bear to part with some of the things we've had for years."

Cassie looked around. She remembered the small, narrow-stemmed vase Mrs. Yashimoto always had on the table. She wondered about the porcelain bowls that were filled with fruit. She thought of the ceramic tea cups they used for meals on the farm. "Will your things be safe?" she wanted to know.

Mrs. Yashimoto shook her head again. "Who knows?" she said. "Anything can happen. Who can say?"

Just then Miko's father entered the kitchen. He smiled as he saw Cassie. "Welcome back, Cassie," he said. "It's nice to see you before we go."

He looked older, thinner, Cassie thought. He also looked worried.

"It's worse than I thought," he said to his wife. "We're getting next to nothing for the tables and lamps. I've been to all the shops near here. Either the dealers don't want them, or they refuse to pay anything like a fair price."

"What did you do?" Mrs. Yashimoto asked.

"I sold them. What else could I do?"

Cassie looked over at Miko. She could feel a growing emptiness in the house like she had felt when they packed up and left Tennessee. But at least then they were moving because her father had wanted to go.

After lunch, Cassie and Miko went outside.

"My father's worried about what's going to happen to the farm when we're gone," Miko said.

"What do you mean?"

"He's afraid other people who've wanted his land for a long time are going to come and take it."

"They can't do that!" Cassie exclaimed.

"My father says they can do whatever they want. It's war. Anything goes. Especially against the Japanese."

"What about the law?"

"The law doesn't seem to help anymore. My father says it's some kind of new law that's making all the Japanese get out.

"At least you're not selling the farm," Cassie said.

"I'd hate to sell it," Miko answered, "but I think my father would if he could. He's put everything he had into it and is scared he may lose it all now. It's just like all the rest of the stuff. He can't get much for it, but it really hurts him to take an unfair price."

"It'll be here when you come back," Cassie said. "I know it will."

"I hope you're right," Miko said. "I hope you're right."

As they talked, the girls wandered past the barn into a field beyond the fence. They headed for a tall oak tree that had been a favorite hiding place before. When Miko's brother, Kenshi, had given them a hard time, they had been able to retreat to the tree, climb half-way up its limbs, and feel the breeze blowing through their hair.

For Cassie, returning to the tree felt like coming home.

Climbing up the bottom branches, she worried for a moment about her leg. She hadn't been up a tree since the accident. But then she told herself that her leg was all right, and the only thing that would hurt it would be if she fell. She resolved to be as careful as she could.

From her viewpoint, perched on a limb, she could see a few of the factories pouring out smoke in one direction, the ugly projects in another, with row after row of the same gray apartments. She hated the way they looked. Quickly she turned and looked the other way. Back on the farm she wanted to keep those areas as distant as she could.

"Are you scared?" she asked Miko.

"Yes."

"I'd be scared too."

"It's not just leaving. It's...it's the worry my mother and father feel. They're afraid of what might happen. They're scared of having to start all over again. They're afraid someone'll get hurt."

"I know."

"I can help pack," Miko went on, "but there's not much more I can do. They don't want to talk about it when we're home alone. Kenshi won't talk to me about it. You're about the only one I can say anything to, and you're not supposed to be here at all."

Cassie felt a funny sense of responsibility, not for herself, but for Miko. "I just wish there was something I could do," she said. She sat swaying on the branch for a while, then remembered that she had been due home several hours ago, and her father would be angry if he found out where she had been. She felt a tightness in her chest as she thought of what he might do. "I'd better go," she said finally. "I wish I could stay, but I've got to go."

37

Miko walked her through a shortcut to the edge of the project. She didn't want to come any farther for fear that Cassie's father might be around and see her. Like Cassie, she was afraid of his temper and knew she had to stay out of his sight.

Rounding the final corner, Cassie saw him sitting on the front steps.

"Where you been, young lady? Your ma and me wanted to go shopping downtown."

"I stayed after school," Cassie said, realizing too late that she was approaching the apartment from the wrong direction.

"I'll bet you did. And what did you do?"

Cassie wasn't sure how much he knew or how much she should say. It was safer to say nothing, she decided. She started to go around him up the stairs, but he stood up and grabbed her arm as she passed.

"I don't believe you. And I want to know where you been."

"Let me go!"

Cassie's mother came to the door. Seeing what was happening, she stepped back.

"I bet I know where you been. Been over with them Japs." When Cassie didn't answer, her father went on. "I thought I told you to stay away. But you don't listen to nothing any more."

Cassie remained silent.

Her father took a deep breath. Cassie could feel him torn between wanting to let her go and needing to say something. The need to respond won out. "I've warned you, Cassie, but you just won't listen. Well, I'm goin' to teach you a lesson once and for all."

"No, Adam. Please." Her mother spoke for the first time.

"You stay out of it, hear? You'll have your go at her when I'm gone. This here's between me and her."

Cassie caught her breath, stifling a sob. Her father hadn't hit her for years, but she could feel it coming. She didn't have long to wait, as the hand not holding her came across and slapped her left cheek. The blow stung, but even worse was the blow to her pride. She'd

38

felt bad enough the whole time she had had been here. The slap reduced her to tears. She thought for a moment of bolting from the house, but dim memories of doing that the day of the accident rattled around in her mind. And anyway, her father still blocked the way. Breaking away, she ran into the house to her room.

Now the tears began to flow. Sobbing on her bed, she felt her pillow become damp but didn't care. Earlier she had been thinking about Miko. Now all thoughts turned back to home, and any mixed feelings Cassie felt about her father vanished. She had been trying to feel better about him ever since she knew he was leaving. Now she could hardly wait for him to go.

CHAPTER 6

Home

Cassie trudged out of the school yard and headed home alone. Turning corners and crossing streets, she kept her eyes out for cars. Memories of the accident lingered on.

She felt lonely, at loose ends, as she had for the several weeks since Miko had gone. She had been quieter in school, so much so that Miss Daniel had asked her what was wrong. Cassie had shrugged off the question, but she knew that Miss Daniel knew what was troubling her. Cassie simply didn't want to talk about it in front of all the other kids.

Leaving the school yard, Cassie wandered toward the apartments in the housing project, past the regular after-school baseball game. Sometimes she wished she could play baseball, but Cassie knew she would never join any game Sam was in, even if she could. Joel saw her and said "Hi." Sam just glared at him.

Walking by herself, without Miko to talk to, Cassie was more conscious of her surroundings. They looked even grungier than before and made her feel desperate to be anywhere else.

Cassie continued to feel the dull ache in her chest that had begun as Miko's family prepared to leave. There was often a lump in her throat, and a tightness farther down. She was afraid to mention it to her mother. She didn't think she was sick and understood the problem; she just didn't know what to do.

The feeling was even worse as she entered her own house. Her mother was working. The day her father had gone off into the Army, her mother had begun to look for work, and had found a job in a shipyard that afternoon.

Her mother was happier than she had ever been. Cassie simply missed her at home when she returned from school. Without even thinking about it, she turned on the radio so she didn't feel alone.

"On the eastern front, the Germans are renewing their offensive against the Russians. Bitter fighting threatens as the Russians refuse to yield to the German advance." Cassie listened to the broadcast for a moment. The war news seemed all the same and was sometimes hard to follow. She was more interested now that her father had become a soldier but couldn't get as excited about military maneuvers as some of the boys at school. Still, she had put up a map with colored pins on it in her room so she could follow what was going on. Red for the Allies, blue for the Axis. Now she tried to think back to what the announcer had said.

Tired of the news, Cassie turned the dial. Music came from the radio, and she felt a little better.

Putting her books on the kitchen table, Cassie went back outside to check the mailbox. There were two letters there—one from her father and one from Miko.

The one from her father was addressed to Nellie Clay. Cassie put it on the table. With trembling hands she opened the letter from Miko to her.

Dear Cassie,

It's been a while since we left, and I've wanted to write to you, but too much has been happening. We are now at Santa Anita racetrack, strange as that seems. My whole family, and lots of other families, met at a church parking lot and then were brought here by bus. I was scared and didn't know where we were going, but my mother told me not to worry, that everything would be all right. That's not so easy. I know she's worried too. And my father is really quiet these days. Right now we're sleeping in an old horse stall. It's not that bad, only it still smells like horses. Kenshi thinks it's an adventure, but I'd rather be home. The food is awful here. But at least our family is together. Kenshi and I have been exploring but haven't found much interesting to see.

I miss you. Please write.

Love,
Miko

After reading the letter a first time, Cassie felt close to her again. She pulled out a school pad and pencil and started to write a response.

After writing "Dear Miko," she didn't know what else to say. Not much had changed at home. Miko knew about her father leaving and her mother going to work. She could write about Miss Daniel and the others at school, Cassie thought, but she wondered if Miko would really be interested in all that now.

Cassie was still thinking about her own letter when her mother came in the door.

"Hello, pumpkin." Nellie walked over to the table and kissed Cassie on the cheek. To Cassie it seemed as though her mother hugged her and kissed her more now that her father was gone. All they had was each other, she guessed. And that was fine with her.

"Hi, Ma. Have a good day?"

"It's hard work, but I love it. I'm tired, but I could do this forever. I'm starting to learn how to use the drill press right now. It's a big machine, but I can handle it. We're cutting holes in sheets of steel to be bolted on the hull of a ship.

"Are you sure you're OK?" Cassie tried to imagine what the tool looked like. It couldn't be anything like the hand drill her father sometimes had used at home.

"I'm strong enough to work it. And if the other women can handle drill presses and riveting guns, I can too."

"What do you do now, anyhow?"

"A bunch of people bring in the steel and line it up on my machine, and I pull the handle down to cut the holes. Then they carry it off, bring another piece in, and I do it again."

Cassie thought for a moment about the shipyard. She had gone down there once just after her mother had started work. She had wanted to see what it was like, and so her mother had taken her to look around. The clanging and hammering of metal echoed through her ears. It was as if a hundred jack hammers were all working around her. She felt the pounding pulse through her mind.

"I wish you were somewhere else. I wish you were doing something different, not so much like a man's work."

"And what's man's work, Cassie?" Her mother smiled slightly.

"I don't know. Like Pa used to do. You know."

"It's different now, Cassie. They need people to work the machines with so many men off fighting in the war. And the people running the factories are finding that we can do the job just as well as the men."

"Yes, but do you like doing that?"

"I love it. I can't type. I don't really want to work as a sales clerk in a store. This feels like real work, like I'm doing something important."

"Is that why you're doing it?"

"That's part of it. I like the paychecks too."

"What would Pa say about this?"

"Does it matter?" Nellie's face clouded a bit as she answered.

"I don't know. Doesn't it?"

"We're here, and he's not. What happens now is between you and me. You may not like what I'm doing, but I need the work, and I like it, and that's that."

Cassie sensed the discussion drawing to a close, but she had something else to ask that was important to her. "Do you miss him, Ma?"

"Of course I do. He's my husband."

"I know that. But do you really miss him?"

Nellie felt herself start to bristle, but she knew what Cassie was asking. "I do, Cassie, I do. You've tangled with him, I know. And I do too, at times. But we've been through a lot together, and I still love him. And I hope you do too."

Cassie squirmed uncomfortably. She did love him. She just didn't know how to show it or talk about it. She decided to change the subject. "Pa wrote you a letter," she said.

Nellie looked at Cassie abruptly. "Where's it at?" she asked.

"Over there." Cassie motioned toward the other side of the table with a nod of her head.

Nellie picked up the envelope, stared at it for a moment, then opened it carefully.

"What's he say?"

Nellie was silent for a moment, then said without looking up, "Let me read it first."

Cassie realized that she hadn't even thought about her father's letter in her excitement over Miko's. She knew that she wasn't to open mail addressed to anyone else, and the envelope had only Nellie's name on it. But she hadn't even wondered what it said or where her father was.

After a few moments, her mother looked up. "He's in England now. Basic training's done, and they shipped him over two weeks ago."

"He liking it there?"

"Seems so. Says he does. Some folks in his company he can't stand. But he was always like that."

"He wanted to go, didn't he?" Cassie asked.

"I guess so. He was restless. He liked the money and the work here. But coming up to Los Angeles made him want to see more things, and he figured it'd be good to go."

As her mother got up to go into the bedroom, she noticed the other envelope on the table. "Who's that from?" she asked.

"Miko."

"What's she say?"

"She's living at a racetrack with lots of other Japanese folks. They're sleeping in a stall. It sounds awful."

Her mother looked at Cassie for a moment. "You know, I always liked Miko. Your pa, he felt different. And I always felt bad when he wouldn't let her come into the house anymore."

Cassie didn't say a word. She hadn't mentioned Miko much to her mother, out of fear that her father might find out about it. She knew her mother was more sympathetic but hadn't wanted to push

44

the issue. Now she felt awkward. Her father was gone. But she wasn't sure how much she could talk to her mother.

Her mother seemed to sense her awkwardness. "It's OK," she said. "This is between you and me. I wish we had talked before. It might have made things easier for all of us. But that's over and done with. I'm just sorry I didn't let you know before how I felt."

"Why didn't you say anything back then?"

"I suppose I was scared of your pa, too. I didn't want to do anything behind his back. He was fixed in his ways. I couldn't see the sense in hassling him, when he was working so hard. After a time I saw how it was hurting you. But by then it was too late."

"I wish you had said something before."

"I do too. All I can say now is I'm sorry."

Her mother drew Cassie to her feet and gave her a big hug. "I wish I could make it different, but I can't. But we can try to do better from now on."

After dinner, Cassie and her mother remained seated at the kitchen table for a while. It helped to talk to her mother. Cassie felt better, more peaceful than she had in a long time.

"Who're you seeing now that Miko's gone?" Nellie asked.

"You knew I was seeing Miko?"

Nellie nodded. "I guessed you must be, though I didn't want to ask. But that still doesn't answer my question."

"There really isn't anyone."

"No one at all?"

"No one like Miko. She was special."

"No one you talk with or play with at school?"

"I was playing jacks with Maria on the playground today. But that was strange. I like her, but she's so quiet I sometimes get the feeling I don't know her at all."

"Who's Maria?"

"Maria Garcia. She's the Mexican girl who was new a couple of months ago. She's in my class."

Cassie looked up and saw her mother catch herself at the mention of the name. "I know who she is," Cassie said finally.

"How do you know?" her mother wanted to know.

"She told me a while back. I guess she felt funny because of her father and the accident. But it's all right. It doesn't bother me. Are you angry?"

Nellie paused for a moment. "No, not really. It's just strange. He came to the hospital, but in a city like this, I never thought our paths would cross again."

"She asked me if I could come over to her house after school some time," Cassie said.

"And what did you say?"

"I said I didn't know."

"Do you want to go?"

"Yes."

"Then why didn't you say so?"

"I...I was afraid of you, and of what Pa might say if you let him know."

Her mother paused, then finally answered. "I told you, everything is between the two of us now," she said. "Go."

CHAPTER 7

Maria's House

At the end of school the next Monday, Cassie waited for Maria by the classroom door.

"Hi, Maria," Cassie said. "I wanted to talk to you for a moment."

"Hi, Cassie," Maria looked at her tentatively. Her eyes scanned Cassie's face. She seemed hopeful yet still shy, Cassie thought.

"I spoke to my mother. She says I can come over to your house. I wondered when you'd like me to come."

Maria brightened. "Soon," she said. "Today I've got to go home and help my mother iron. How about tomorrow?"

"Fine," Cassie answered. "I'm not doing anything, anyway. My father's off in the Army, and my mother's working until late afternoon. Anytime's OK."

"Me too. My mother's been wanting to meet you. And my father's...." She broke off and stopped speaking.

Cassie looked at her expectantly. "Does he still feel funny about...."

Maria nodded.

"It's all over. And I'm fine. Look at me. Good as new."

"I know. But for him it's not so easy. He still has nightmares about that day."

"Don't worry," Cassie said. "It's all right."

Cassie went off in one direction, Maria in another. Cassie found herself skipping as she headed home. It'll be nice tomorrow, she thought as she turned the first corner into the project. I haven't played with anyone since Miko went away.

The next noontime, Cassie waited for Maria again by the schoolroom door. "You lead the way," she said. "You don't live far, do you?"

"No, just on the other side of the project. It's a fifteen minute walk."

"How long have you been living here?" Cassie asked as they left the school yard. "You started school when I was in the hospital. But where were you before that?"

"We came up from Mexico a couple of years ago. My father came to work in the fields, picking crops. But he hated doing that. I hated it too. We lived in one place, then another, moving all the time. And my mother told him we couldn't go on that way."

"So what happened then?"

"We moved to East Los Angeles. There were lots of Mexicans there. My father got a job as a janitor in a small company, and we stayed in one apartment for a year."

"And after that?"

"My father heard about new defense factories here and got a job in the steel plant."

"Are there many other Mexicans here in the project?" Cassie couldn't remember seeing many Mexican kids in school.

"A few. My mother and father argued about that. My father said he needed a better job. My mother was afraid we'd be all alone here, and people wouldn't be nice. She liked the place we used to live in, 'cause all the neighbors spoke Spanish. And she had friends there."

"How 'bout you?"

"I liked it too. I had a friend there, but I haven't seen her much since we left. It's...it's been hard here."

"I know what you mean." Cassie thought about her own longing for home. "When we came from Tennessee, I couldn't stand it. It was OK once I met Miko—you remember Miko—but then they took her whole family away. And it's been feeling just like it did before."

"I saw you go home with her every day. I wished I had a friend like that here."

"That was all right for a while. But then my father wouldn't let her in the house anymore, and I had to see her when he wasn't around."

"Why'd he do that?"

"He didn't like anybody who was, you know, different. And after Pearl Harbor, it got worse."

Maria was silent for a moment. Softly she said, "I feel different here."

Cassie felt that tightness in her chest again. Had she said something wrong? And how could she make it better. She walked on for a moment, looking at her feet. "My father didn't like much of anybody who seemed any different from him," she said finally.

"I know," Maria said. "My father told me about the hospital. That's why he felt a little funny about your coming over."

"But my father's gone now," Cassie continued. "And my mother doesn't care." She paused for a moment. "And I don't care."

The girls walked on silently for a few minutes. Cassie kicked a small pebble over toward Maria's feet. Maria knocked it back with her shoe. They kept that up for half a block until they came to Maria's home, a gray, wooden apartment that looked just like Cassie's.

"Mama. We're here. Cassie's with me." Maria entered the front door first, and led Cassie to the kitchen.

"Hello, Cassie." A woman with short black hair and friendly dark eyes greeted her in English, but with a heavy Mexican accent. She sounded different from Miko's mother, Cassie thought.

"Hello." Cassie wasn't sure quite what to say. Everyone seemed awkward, herself included. "It's nice to be here."

"It's nice you come. Maria talks about you many times. Come. Sit down."

Maria whispered something to her mother. Mrs. Garcia nodded as she turned and went over to the sink to get some glasses. "My mother's promised to try to speak only English while you're here,"

Maria said to Cassie while her mother was away. "She can do it, but she says it feels strange."

Mrs. Garcia came back with the glasses. "Milk? Juice?" she asked.

"Juice," the girls answered together as they sat down at the table.

Cassie looked at the plate in front of her. There were some funny, crusty brown beans, some red peppers, and a lot of other stuff she didn't recognize. Gingerly, she picked up her fork when the others did and began to eat.

Maria watched her and smiled. "You haven't had Mexican food before?"

Cassie shook her head.

"I hope you like it. Some of it's a little spicy. But the beans are really good."

Cassie remembered the first time she had eaten raw fish at Miko's. Just the thought of it had been awful, but once she had gotten it down, it hadn't been so bad. This couldn't be any worse, she thought. Nothing like this in Tennessee. But then, everything was different here. "I'm willing to try new things," she said with her mouth full. Something that looked and tasted like ground hamburger was actually good.

Maria looked over and smiled. Then, glancing at her mother, she asked, "Where's Ricardo?"

Her mother's face clouded. "He went back to East Los Angeles this morning. He's been spending more and more time there."

"Who's Ricardo?" Cassie asked.

"My brother. He's sixteen. I'll tell you about him later."

Cassie, Maria, and Mrs. Garcia continued eating. When they were done the girls got up to help clear the table. "Thank you. It's all right. I'll do it today," Mrs. Garcia said.

"It's all done," Maria answered, as she took the last plates over to the sink.

"Let's go to my room." Maria took Cassie to a small bedroom, which had a narrow bed, a three-drawer dresser, and a faded red rug.

It was much like her own room, Cassie thought. Simple, sparse. Somehow it felt good to see someone else in a situation just like her own. "What's Ricardo like?" Cassie asked as they sat down together on the bed.

"Mean," Maria said. He does whatever he wants. Sometimes, like today, he just skips school.

"What's he do?"

"I don't know for sure. He's been hanging out with a bunch of kids from our neighborhood when we lived there. They call themselves the White Fence Gang. Some of them tattooed a small cross and some dots on their left hand just above the thumb. Ricardo didn't do that, but he would sometimes draw it in with black ink, to make it look like a tattoo."

Cassie grimaced. She didn't like the idea of tattooing anything.

"He also sometimes wears clothes they call a 'zoot suit,'" Maria went on. "You know, with a long coat and tight pants at the bottom."

Cassie didn't really know what a zoot suit was but didn't want to ask. It was something Mexican, she supposed. It sounded weird.

"What does he do like that," she asked.

"I don't know. Just wanders around."

Cassie wondered what Ricardo was like. She'd get to see him sometime, she supposed.

Cassie and Maria wandered down the front stairs and out of the house. "Come," Maria said. "I'll show you my secret place."

They headed along the street Maria lived on, passing house after house that looked the same.

"This way," Maria said as they turned to the left near the outskirts of the project. Then they were off in a field, like the one on the way to Miko's farm, but in a different direction. Off in the distance, a factory spewed out smoke, but they turned the other way and headed for a line of trees. Nearby was some heavy brush. Pushing some green vines away, Maria made her way into a small thicket.

"No one else knows about this," she said. "'Least no one I know. I come here when I want to be all alone. You're the first person I've ever brought here."

"It's neat." Cassie sat down on the grass in one corner of the thicket. The shrubbery was so thick you couldn't see out. It was dark, with just a bit of light coming in through the branches and leaves. It smelled fresh, like she remembered back in Tennessee. "I like it," she said after a while. "I used to have a place like this back home."

"You miss home, too?"

"All the time."

"Think you'll ever get back there?"

"I don't know. I don't think my father'll want to go back. He never did well back there, and he was much happier here before he left. Who knows what'll happen after the war's over."

"My mother'd like to go back home. All her relatives are still back in Mexico. But this is the first decent job my father's had. Like in your family, I don't see him wanting to go back."

"What's your father like?" Cassie asked.

Maria thought about that for a moment. "He's kind of quiet, I guess. He listens when we talk. He didn't like living where we used to. I think he thought we'd never get out if we stayed there. He wants us to go to school, and do something. That's why he's worried about Ricardo."

"Will I get to see him today?" Cassie asked.

"I don't think so. He won't get home until dinner time. You'll probably be going before then."

"Oh, my gosh," Cassie said. "I told my mother I'd be home to help fix supper. I'd better be on my way."

Maria nodded. "It's about that time. I've got to help at home, too." She paused. "I've had a nice day. I hope you can come back another time."

"I'd like that," Cassie said. "You can come over to my house, too. Nobody'll be home in the afternoon, with my mother working. And with my father away, anybody's welcome."

Maria looked up. "Your mother won't mind?"

"No," Cassie said. "She'd be glad for you to come over. She'd even like to meet you sometime when she gets home."

Crawling out of the thicket, Cassie left Maria when they reached the road. A couple of boys playing marbles looked up at her as she passed. One of them waved. Cassie barely saw them. For the first time since Miko left, she felt better as she headed home.

CHAPTER 8

Shopping

"Ma, can Maria come over tomorrow after school?" Cassie and her mother were sitting at the kitchen table eating dinner. Cassie had seen a good deal of Maria in the past few months. She had found the new friend she'd been looking for, and the two girls had been back and forth to one another's homes several times each week.

"Of course," Nellie answered.

"Can she stay for supper too?"

"Why not? In fact, I've got to work late tomorrow. Why don't the two of you do the shopping and cook dinner for the three of us?"

"Aw, Ma."

"No, I think it's a good idea. I'll give you the ration books, and you can get what you need. I should have done the shopping by now, but I've been too busy this week. They're asking us to work overtime whenever we can."

"But I don't know which coupons to use, or what to give the people at the store. What if I do something wrong?"

"I'll show you the proper coupons tonight and tell you what we need. It's time you were doing some of this. Why, when I was your age...."

"OK, OK."

Cassie and her mother cleared the table, then sat down together with the ration book for sugar. The cover was light brown, the color of a paper bag, with imprints of eagles in red. The stamps themselves had a drawing of a woman on a red, white, and blue background, with the dates they could be used and the number of pounds they could buy printed in the middle.

"I don't know why we have to use these silly coupons anyway," Cassie said.

"It's to make stuff go around so everyone can get something."

54

"Why isn't there enough for everybody?"

"'Cause the factories are all making things for the war."

"Why do they need sugar?"

"Soldiers got to eat too, Cassie. This war's a big operation. Lots of stuff is in short supply."

"I'm gettin' sick and tired of all the shortages, Ma. You know what happened yesterday? Maria and me, we went over to Mr. Cooper's candy store by the school. And he'd raised the price of the candy. Said with sugar scarce, his cost was going up. You'd given me a dime, and it wasn't enough."

"That's too bad, pumpkin, but it's something we've got to live with for now. That's why we've got the ration books. Here, let me show you which coupon you'll need for the meat."

After school the next day, Cassie and Maria had lunch at Cassie's house, then started for the row of shops at the end of the project.

"Race you to the corner." Challenging Maria, Cassie took off immediately. She was running normally now, with no trace of a limp. It had taken a year, but her leg had healed nicely. It was good to feel free on her feet.

Maria caught up quickly. Like Cassie, she was slender and swift. She reached over, grabbed Cassie's blouse from behind where it had pulled out from her skirt, and forced her to slow down.

"Wait up, wait up," she laughed as she gasped for breath.

"Make me," Cassie gasped, as she pulled away again.

Maria caught up once more, and this time made Cassie pause. "How about telling me where we're going?"

"Shopping for dinner."

"Where abouts?"

"Butcher shop first. Bakery next. Then the vegetable wagon back near home."

"What's for supper?"

"My ma said to get stuff for stew."

"Yuk."

"Come on. It's as good as that glop I eat at your house."

"Don't let my mother hear you say that."

"I won't. But don't you complain either."

A few more blocks and they reached the butcher store. Inside they found a crowd around the meat case. It would be some time until it was their turn.

Cassie saw Joel, her friend from school. He'd been even nicer to her recently, saying hello when many of the other boys wouldn't. And the other day, he'd been in the candy store when she hadn't had enough money and gave her a piece of his own.

"Hi, Joel. What're you doing here?" Cassie spoke, as Maria stood silent, looking down.

"Hi, Cassie. Hi, Maria. My mother asked me to buy some hamburger if they have any."

Cassie was glad Joel was there. She just wished Maria would say something.

All three watched as the butcher helped the first woman in line. She wanted some kind of pot roast, and had the necessary coupons, but still the butcher hesitated.

"What's the matter? Ain't you got the roast?"

"Not today, Mrs. Hawkins. We're running short of everything."

"Who you savin' it for, anyhow?"

"Come on, Mrs. Hawkins. You know we don't keep anything back."

"I've a good mind to stay right here and watch to make sure no one else don't get it neither."

"What's going on?" Maria whispered to Cassie.

"My ma says sometimes the butcher keeps special cuts for his best customers, or for people who'll buy some of his other stuff," Joel said, before she could answer. "She says it's part of what they call the black market."

"Black market?" Maria looked puzzled, and her voice became louder.

"Shhhh," Cassie whispered. "Everybody'll hear you."

"Sorry," Maria whispered back. "But what's a black market?"

"It's where you can get things you're not supposed to have by paying a little more." This time Cassie answered. Just then they reached the front of the line, and Mr. Hawkins stared at them. Had he heard what they were saying? Cassie wondered.

"Can I help you?" Mr. Hawkins spoke directly to Cassie.

"I'd like some meat for stew."

"How much?"

"About half a pound."

"You have coupons?"

"Here." Cassie thrust the ration book up at him.

The butcher reached for the book, took the necessary coupon, and returned it to Cassie. Then he went to the stew tray and took out several chunks of red meat.

"My ma said to ask you for less fat than you gave us last time."

Mr. Hawkins grimaced as a number of the other women waiting in line smiled.

"You'll take what I give you. If your mother don't like it, she can come in herself to complain."

"She's working." Cassie was going to say something more, but thought better of it and kept quiet.

Mr. Hawkins handed her a wrapped package, took her dollar bill and gave her change. "Next," he said as the girls left the store, nodding good-bye to Joel as they went.

"Do you like him?" Cassie reddened as Maria spoke.

"I guess so."

"Why?"

"'Cause he seems nice." She paused. "Not like Sam." Cassie wanted to say more but was embarrassed. Some of the girls were starting to talk about boys, but she'd never said much. Maybe another time she'd be able to talk to Maria about this, she thought.

Cassie and Maria went next door to the bakery for fresh bread, then headed back toward Cassie's home. As they approached the apartment, they stopped at a rickety, rusted vegetable cart parked around the corner.

"Hello, Mr. Florentini," Cassie said.

"Ah, my little pet with the sore leg."

"It's all right now, Mr. Florentini. You remember Maria, don't you?"

"Hello, Maria. Nice to see you again. And what can I do for you ladies today?"

"My ma wants some carrots and celery sticks and potatoes for stew."

"Good as done." The old Italian vegetable peddler picked out the things Cassie wanted. "Only the very best for my little pet."

Cassie took the package, paid for it with some of her change, and left with a smile. "See you next week," she said as she and Maria headed home.

"That was nice, girls," Nellie said as they finished dinner. The three of them were sitting around the table. No one was ready to clear the dishes yet.

"We told you what we did this afternoon, Ma. How was your day?"

"It's tougher than it used to be. Overtime's starting to get me down. Money's nice, but I'm getting tired."

Cassie wondered if it was worry about Pa that was making her mother tired. She wasn't sure. "You didn't used to complain," she said.

"I know. But that was then."

Cassie thought her mother was going to say something more, but she changed her mind, then got up and started to clear the table. "Bring me those cans, will you, Maria," she said. "Cassie, would you wash them and I'll flatten them."

As Cassie handed her the clean cans, she peeled the labels off, removed the remaining end from each, and flattened the cylinders with her foot.

"What're you doing?" Maria asked.

"Doesn't your ma do this in your house?"

Maria shook her head.

"I'm saving the tin. Recycling it for the war effort. Like in those advertisements you see, telling you to save all your used up stuff. It's a pain sometimes, but it's worth it, I guess."

Maria took one of the remaining tin cans and crushed it underneath her foot. "Where do I put it now?"

Nellie nodded her head toward a small cardboard box in the corner of the kitchen. "Metals over there. Fats from cooking here on the counter."

"Does saving all this stuff really make a difference?" Cassie asked.

"I don't know. It must. And it makes us feel good to do it," her mother answered.

With the dishes done, Maria looked at the kitchen clock. "It's getting late," she said. "My mother'll be wondering about me."

"I'll walk you part way home," Cassie volunteered.

"That'll be nice. Thanks very much for dinner, Mrs. Clay."

"Any time, Maria. It's nice having you here. Cassie likes it. And I do, too."

Together the two girls left the house. It was starting to get dark, but Cassie didn't care. As she had gotten to know Maria better, she was feeling better about the neighborhood.

"I like it with your ma," Maria said as they turned the corner. "She makes me feel at home. It's good to get away from my house sometimes."

"What's wrong?" Cassie asked.

"My brother. He's starting to get into more trouble with his gang."

"What kind of trouble?"

"Fighting and stuff like that."

"Bad?"

Maria nodded. "I'll tell you about it next time. I've got to go." With that she turned one last corner, waved goodbye to Cassie, and began to run toward home.

CHAPTER 9

Violence

"Blow out your candles, Maria." Mrs. Garcia was urging her along. It was mid-May, and Maria was celebrating her eleventh birthday.

Cassie watched as Maria took a deep breath, then blew out all the flames. She'd been spending more and more time with Maria, either at the Garcia home or her own, and was included in the birthday celebration.

"Can I open my presents now?"

"Of course," her mother answered.

From her pocket Cassie pulled out a small box she had wrapped herself earlier in the day. Smiling in anticipation of Maria's reaction, she handed it over to her friend. Maria took the box and opened it first.

"Oooo. They're beautiful." She removed a pair of tiny gold earrings.

Cassie just smiled.

"How did you....Where did you get them?"

Cassie continued to smile without saying a word.

Aware of the cost, Mr. Garcia frowned slightly. "They're lovely, Cassie. But you shouldn't have."

Not expecting this reaction, Cassie felt her face cloud. "I wanted to. I've been saving money Ma gives me from time to time for doing chores. This is what I wanted to spend it on."

"Thanks, Cassie." Maria hugged her, and suddenly it was all right.

Mrs. Garcia gave Maria a bright red blouse she had made. Her father gave her a small mirror inlaid in wood he had picked out specially for her. Only her brother was empty-handed. Cassie wasn't sure whether Ricardo had forgotten Maria's birthday, or just

61

refused to celebrate it. He sat by himself in a corner of the living room. He wasn't usually around when Cassie was over, and almost never spoke to her. She wondered about him, and was even more curious today. She resolved to ask Maria about him when they were alone.

"Time for cake and ice cream." Mrs. Garcia was speaking English more easily since Cassie had been coming around. She no longer felt reluctant to try to talk, and the more she spoke, the better she became.

"Mmmm, good," Cassie said as she took a first bite of the cake. It was rich, filled with cream, unlike anything she had tasted before. She wondered what her mother would make for her birthday next month.

"Let's go for a walk." Maria made the suggestion as the celebration wound down.

Nodding, Cassie followed her friend outside. "What's with Ricardo?" she asked as they left the house.

"He's angry."

"Why?"

"There's been trouble recently between Mexicans and sailors in town. I heard my father talking about it."

"What's going on?"

"Down in Venice last week a bunch of sailors attacked some Mexican high school kids. The sailors thought someone had been stabbed and went after anyone they could find. Then the police arrested the kids."

"What does that have to do with Ricardo? Was he there?"

"No. But he says there's going to be more trouble, and the sailors better watch out."

"What does your father say?"

"He's upset. He's afraid that any trouble with Mexicans'll make it harder for all of us."

"Has he talked to Ricardo?"

"No one can talk to Ricardo. He won't listen."

❖   ❖   ❖

Three weeks later, Cassie was back at Maria's house. Maria had invited her to spend the night. It was the first time Cassie was staying overnight at a friend's since she'd been at Miko's a year and a half ago.

In the Garcia home, Cassie knew something was wrong. Maria looked pale, she thought.

"Evening, Mr. Garcia," Cassie said, as Maria's father entered the living room.

"Hello, Cassie."

His brow seemed furrowed, and his smile seemed forced.

"Where's Ricardo?" Cassie whispered to Maria as they went into the kitchen to get a snack.

"I don't know. Out somewhere."

"Is that why your father looks worried?"

"I think so. A few nights ago some more sailors tore the zoot suits I was telling you about off some Mexican kids sitting in a theater."

"Were they hurt?"

"I think so. But nothing happened to the sailors. My father said the police just let them go."

"Was Ricardo there?"

"No. But he says his friends'll get revenge."

"I think I see why your father's upset."

"Only problem is, there's nothing he can do. He'd like to tell Ricardo not to go downtown, but Ricardo won't listen. So he's just hoping things don't get too bad."

Later that evening, after Cassie and Maria had gone to bed, they heard a pounding at the door.

"What's that?" Cassie asked as she awoke, worried at the sound.

"I'm not sure."

Leaving the bedroom in their pajamas, Cassie and Maria followed Mr. Garcia to the door. There, bloody and battered, Ricardo stood leaning against a Mexican friend.

"Ricardo!" Mr. Garcia reached out to grab him and helped him inside as quickly as he could.

Cassie watched, horrified. She had never seen anyone so badly beaten up. Ricardo's jaw sagged, his left eye was black, and his right arm dangled by his side. It looked broken, Cassie thought. His clothes were in shreds. His long jacket was gone, and his narrow-cuffed trousers were little better than ripped rags.

Cassie couldn't understand what was going on. No one was speaking English. Spanish echoed around her, as Maria's mother and father tried to find out what had happened. Maria stood back with Cassie, eyes large, not saying a word.

Cassie wanted to ask questions too but thought better of it. Maria'll tell me later when she can, she said to herself.

Gently, Mrs. Garcia removed Ricardo's bloody clothes, first his shirt, then his pants. She said little as she bathed him and sponged a gash on his good arm. Mr. Garcia stood back, helping her when she asked, moving Ricardo so she could reach behind.

Cassie felt sick to her stomach. "Maybe I'd better go," she whispered to Maria.

"Please don't." Maria's whisper was frantic. "I...I don't know what I'd do without you."

"Won't I be in the way?"

"No. They'll be so busy with Ricardo that they won't notice you or me."

Cassie and Maria continued to watch. Ricardo's friend spoke briefly to Mr. and Mrs. Garcia, telling them what had happened. Maria leaned closer, anxious to hear.

Finally Mrs. Garcia finished cleaning Ricardo. Cassie listened uncomprehendingly to the Spanish, then heard a word that sounded like hospital. Images of her own experience flashed through her mind.

Mr. Garcia went outside and started up the truck. Then he and his wife and the friend lifted Ricardo and helped him out of the house. The truck sped off into the darkness.

Cassie was grateful when Maria nodded that they could retreat to her room. With the door safely closed behind them, Cassie began pumping Maria to find out more. "Where did Ricardo get beat up?" she wanted to know.

"He was back in East L.A. Back where we used to live."

"What happened?"

"Sailors beat up on him."

"Why?"

"Who knows. Ricardo's friend didn't say."

"Come on. Tell me what you know. I couldn't understand anything in there. You know that."

Maria still looked a little dazed. "I'm sorry. Somehow I thought you knew."

Cassie shook here head.

"Just like before. Sailors were looking for trouble. Whenever they saw any Mexicans, they'd rip off their clothes."

"Why?" Cassie wanted to know again.

"Seems like they didn't like anyone different. And I guess the zoot suits made them stand out. People like Ricardo never had a chance."

"You're no different from other people."

"Doesn't seem to matter." Maria fell silent for a moment. Then she went on. "It's·just like with Miko," she said.

"What do you mean?"

"Some folks hated the Japanese and were happy to get rid of them. Now that they're gone, people can gang up on someone else."

Cassie felt uncomfortable with the conversation. She knew Maria wasn't referring to her but was still uneasy. Changing the subject, she asked, "Is Ricardo going to be OK?"

"I think so. My mother thinks his arm is broken. Did you see the way it hung by his side?"

Cassie nodded. "Where's your father taking him?"

"To the hospital. But he didn't want to go to the hospital near the project."

"Why not?"

"'Cause there aren't a whole lot of Mexicans around here, and he's afraid they might give him a hard time. He's going to drive back toward town."

"Is your father mad?"

"More upset, I think. He's been worried something like this was going to happen. I think he's afraid it's not over, that it's going to get worse."

"Can't you just stay out of the way?"

"That won't do. My father really wants us to work hard and be like other folks. Now it's going to be even harder."

"Is that why you asked me to come over here?" Almost as soon as she spoke, Cassie regretted her question. She felt even worse as she saw tears come to Maria's eyes.

"I'm sorry I said that. I didn't mean it. I'm just confused. Sometimes I don't understand what's going on."

"My father's proud of being Mexican but wants to be more than a field worker or a janitor. He's got dreams. Yes, I guess he is glad to have you come here. But he also really likes you. And somehow, it makes him forget the accident a year and a half ago."

Cassie nodded.

"I'm just glad you come over, for me. It was so lonely before. It's better now. I hope you know that."

Cassie nodded again. She reached over and touched Maria gently on the arm. "I was lonely before, too. Real lonely. It's not so bad for me now either."

When they finally turned out the light, Cassie tossed and turned, unable to sleep. Images of Ricardo flashed through her mind. Hospital scenes returned for the first time in months. She wondered if he was in a bed in a ward like the one where she had been. She still felt vaguely queasy as she thought of his bloody face and battered arm. Try as she might, she couldn't understand the violence she had seen.

CHAPTER 10

Letters

"Hi, Ma. I'm home." Cassie opened the front door as she greeted her mother, then stopped to pick up two letters in the mailbox outside.

It was summer now, and Cassie had plenty of free time. With her mother still working, she was almost entirely on her own. She filled up the days playing with Maria whenever she could, or reading quietly by herself. Today she had been over at the Garcia home since early morning. Mrs. Garcia was teaching the two girls how to sew. Cassie's mother didn't have time for sewing anymore, and Cassie was glad to learn how to use the machine. Just this afternoon, she had begun work on a pale-blue cotton blouse. She had thought of staying longer but had come back to see if her mother had returned. Nellie had been having back trouble and had planned to leave the shipyard at 3:00 P.M. to see a doctor. She'd said she'd be home in the late afternoon.

"Here's a letter from Pa," Cassie said. As she handed it over to her mother, she looked more closely at the other envelope. It was addressed to her. There was no name on it, but Cassie knew immediately from the handwriting that it was from Miko.

Her heart pounded as she tore the envelope open. She hadn't heard from Miko in months. She had been spending so much time with Maria, she hadn't even thought about Miko recently. She had written to Miko once or twice and had received an occasional letter in return. She hadn't heard from her in nearly a year though, and had almost begun to forget how close they had once been.

The letter was written on a plain piece of white paper. Cassie felt that same old lump rise in her throat as she read:

Dear Cassie:

It's been a long time, I know, but I still think of you often. It's terrible here in Utah. Santa Anita was bad enough, but Topaz is even worse. In the summer it's hot, often with an awful wind. It's dusty, with few trees like back home.

We live in a single room, with creaky cots for each of us. Each bed has only a single set of sheets, and one blanket. The room has almost no other furniture. There is one bare light bulb that hangs from the ceiling, and that's all. I try to read at night, but can't if everyone else wants to go to sleep.

My mother wants to cook, but she can't. Everybody eats together. It's sometimes hard to feel like a family here.

A while after we got here, an old man was walking near the outer fence and didn't hear a sentry tell him to stop. The sentry killed him. Some people wanted to fight back, but my father said there was nothing we could do. We simply hope the war will be over soon.

I wonder what you're doing now, and whether I will ever see you again. I hope so.

Love,
Miko

Cassie put the letter down. She didn't know how to deal with it. Miko had been so close, but now seemed so far away. The letter brought her closer. But still Cassie didn't know what to do. She felt just like she had when the first letter had come. What could she write to Miko to make her feel better? She could tell Miko what she was doing, she supposed. But would that help? Should she talk about Maria? Wouldn't that just make her feel bad? Cassie felt confused. She wanted to help, but how?

Troubled, she went over to her mother in the other room. She had finished her letter, too, and was staring off into space. She didn't hear Cassie come in.

"What's Pa say this time?"

"Not too much. He's off in Italy now. Fighting's been hard, but it's going OK."

"Is he in any danger?"

"I don't know. He doesn't say."

"Does he like it there?"

"It's funny. I don't think anyone likes fighting the way they are. But I think he's still excited about being over there. He never thought he'd see that part of the world."

"Does he miss you, Ma?"

Her mother's face clouded.

"He does. But you know your pa. He doesn't say much about how he feels. I wish he did, but it's just not his way."

Cassie understood. She had often wished her father could be more expressive. She hadn't realized her mother had felt the same thing.

"You still missing him, Ma?"

Her mother was silent for a moment. "I am," she said. "I really am. I miss having him around. I wish I could share how I feel with him. I like talking to you and all that, Cass, but it's not always the same as having another grownup around. Someone who can hold you when you need it. But...."

"But what?"

"But it's a whole lot easier just living here with you. And working. I don't know how your pa's going to take to my working when he comes back. He didn't want me to go to work in the first place, remember? All I know is, I'm not giving it up."

Cassie didn't know what to say. She knew she ought to want to know how her father was. Yet, in fact, she was still glad he was away. Right now, she just wanted to talk to her mother about Miko and her letter but didn't know how to bring it up, especially when her mother was talking about herself.

Her mother made it easier for her. "You got a letter too, Cassie. Who's yours from?"

"Miko."

"Where's she at now?"

"Utah. Camp called Topaz."

"Her whole family there?"

"Yes."

70

"What's she say?"

"It's awful there, Ma. The place sounds dry and bare. The family's living in one room. They're really unhappy. I don't know how they can stand it. It's like they're in prison."

Her mother frowned as Cassie paused for a moment.

Cassie continued. "Miko says people are kept behind a fence. Sentries make sure they can't get out. And she said one old man got killed when he didn't hear the guard call out. Why're they doing that, Ma? What're they trying to do?"

"I wish I knew, Cassie. Sometimes the government does strange things."

"When will they get out?"

"I don't know."

"Is there anything we can do, Ma?"

"I doubt it."

"It makes me feel all funny inside."

"What do you mean?"

"I feel like why should she be there, and I'm not. And I wonder how I'd feel if I were in the camp." Cassie paused for a moment. "I guess I feel bad too 'cause I haven't written to her much. But I don't know what to say."

"Anything'll help."

"I know, Ma. But I just don't know what to write."

"You know, Cassie, you're a funny girl. I look at you and sometimes you're bubbly and silly and full of fun, and sometimes you have a kind of sadness in your eyes. I remember more of the bubbly back home. Maybe I'm just dreaming about what it was like. I don't know. But I don't remember you all that sad before we came here."

"I feel that, Ma. It's like there are two of me. I call the happy one Cassie. Cassie was doing better when Miko was around. And Cassie's the one that plays hopscotch and runs around with Maria. The other one I call Claytie. Claytie's lonely. And confused.

Claytie did more stuff when Pa was around. Cassie was scared to jump and skip in the house when he was here."

"There's nothing wrong with Claytie, Cassie," Nellie said. "That quietness is often nice. Don't drive it out."

"I know, Ma. But I still like Cassie better."

"I'll bet you do."

"Cassie came home from Maria's. But Claytie got to reading Miko's letter. And I don't know where Cassie went."

Cassie suddenly felt very tired. Still troubled by Miko's letter, she went into her own room.

The next day, Maria came by in the morning. Cassie greeted her as she entered the house.

Maria looked at Cassie. "What's wrong?"

"Wrong?" Cassie looked puzzled.

"You look like something's bothering you. What happened?"

"I got a letter from Miko. Her family's having a hard time. I guess it makes me feel funny. Kind of like I felt when I was at your house and Ricardo got beat up."

"I never knew Miko well. I saw her with you in class. And she was nice to me when we had to do something together in school. But I never talked to her much."

"She was a little like you. Or I think she was. At least I felt good with her like I feel with you."

"Why're you feeling bad right now?"

"I don't know. I guess I wish there was something I could do. But I'm having trouble even writing back."

"Why?"

"She's so far away. I don't know what to say. You're here, and I guess I don't need her like before. And that makes me feel bad."

Maria looked down at the ground. "I don't know what I can say. But I do think you should try to do something."

"That's what my mother says."

"Miko was pretty important to you, wasn't she?"

Cassie nodded.

"Well, then, you've got to do something."

"That makes me feel a whole lot better." Cassie's voice sounded deliberately sarcastic.

"I'm sorry. I don't know what else to say. I feel funny enough talking about Miko anyway."

"I know. I suppose I shouldn't even have mentioned it to you. But you asked. And I tried talking to my ma last night, but I'm not sure how much that helped."

The girls left the house and were heading toward the street as they continued to talk. Both hardly noticed the blue sky or faint breeze.

"Do you talk to your mother much?" Maria changed the subject.

"More since my father's gone."

"Does she listen to you?"

"Sometimes. Sometimes it's real good. Other times she just seems to be thinking about herself."

"Who does she talk to?"

"Sadie. She and Sadie got real close once Pa left. It's good for her to have a friend. She needs one, too."

"She worried about your father?"

"I think so. She's scared he won't come back, and she wonders what she'll do. And then sometimes she's scared he will come back and not like what's happening to her."

"What do you mean?"

"Like working and deciding what she wants to do and all that. Pa always made her feel like there wasn't much she could do by herself."

"I wish I could talk to my mother like you do. She's around all the time, more than your mother. And she's always cooking and sewing and doing things for me, but I still can't tell her how I feel."

"Why not?"

73

"It's like I've got a whole life outside the house that she doesn't share."

"I've got that, too. My mother doesn't see what goes on at school or wherever else I am."

"No, it's different. Maybe 'cause she still feels more comfortable speaking Spanish. Maybe 'cause she's worried about Ricardo. I don't know. But it's like there's a whole part of me she'll never know."

"Does that bother you?"

"Sometimes. It'd bother me more if I couldn't talk to you."

"It's funny. I was just telling Ma about two different parts of me last night. A little like what you're saying only different. But I don't know how much she understood."

Both girls fell silent as they scuffled their sandals in the dust by the side of the road. Maria picked up a stick and began tracing designs in the dirt. Cassie watched what she was doing. Maria looked as if she wanted to say something but was afraid to get it out.

Finally she spoke. "Write to Miko, Cassie. It's none of my business, I guess. But it'll help her and you."

Cassie looked at her without saying a word. Then she nodded and sat down.

CHAPTER 11

Casualty

Cassie was the first one home. It was mid-afternoon as she arrived. She was twelve now, feeling older all the time. School was still in session, but the summer vacation was not far away. Cassie was more than ready for the time off.

Bounding up the stairs, she first noticed the Western Union delivery man standing on the porch. As she stopped by the front door, he handed her a telegram. It was addressed to Mrs. Adam Clay.

Cassie wasn't sure what to do. They hadn't gotten many telegrams before. Cassie knew that she wasn't supposed to open mail addressed to someone else, yet a telegram seemed different. She sensed it was something important and felt she ought to know what it was.

Taking a deep breath, she opened the envelope and began to read. The telegram was short and to the point. "I deeply regret to inform you that Private Adam Clay, US35764128, was killed in Rome on June 4, 1944." It was signed by someone called the Adjutant General, with a name she didn't know.

Cassie gasped. Not believing the message, she read it through again. Then she sat down on the porch and began to cry.

She hadn't really missed her father at first, but in the past year that had begun to change. He'd even begun to write to her, and she had looked forward to his letters. She felt better about him than she had before and was starting to imagine having him home again. Recently, she'd begun to follow the path of General Mark Clark's Fifth Army as it moved up Italy. The war had become more real as she had moved the colored marking pins along the map of the boot-shaped country in her room. She remembered when the Army had entered Rome not long ago. She had never suspected that her father wouldn't survive.

Cassie didn't know what to do. Her mother wouldn't be home for a couple of hours. She could try to reach her by phone, she supposed, but that was hard, and not always possible. The shipyard was never eager to pull someone away from work, least of all for a phone call. Cassie wasn't sure she was up to trying to get through, but she knew she had to talk to someone.

She went inside, left the telegram on the kitchen table, then turned around and went out the front door. Without being quite sure where she was going, she headed toward the far end of the project where Maria lived. Maria remained as close as ever, and the Garcia family had become important to her, too.

Halfway there, Cassie broke into a run. She felt a strange terror sweep over her. She was scared and didn't know why. She wanted to scream but couldn't. She needed someone nearby.

Coming closer to Maria's house, Cassie tripped over a curb and went sprawling on the ground. Her bare knee scraped along the ground and began to bleed. Her hands were covered with dust. Cassie barely felt a thing. Picking herself up, she brushed off her hands, patted her knee with the bottom of her skirt, and began to run again.

As she reached Maria's house, Cassie knocked, struggling to catch her breath.

"Why, Cassie. Hello." Mrs. Garcia answered the door.

Cassie still couldn't say a word.

"Come in, come in." Mrs. Garcia could see with one glance that something was wrong, and took Cassie's arm as she led her into the house. "What's the matter, Cassie?"

Maria came into the living room. Her face brightened as she saw Cassie. It darkened as she looked into her eyes.

"What's happened?"

Cassie began to sob. "My father. He's dead. He was killed in Rome."

Maria went pale. She reached out to Cassie. "Does your mother know?"

Cassie shook her head.

"Where is she now?"

"At work," Cassie said, between sobs.

Mrs. Garcia put her arms around Cassie and held her tight. It felt good. Gently Mrs. Garcia rocked back and forth, her hand stroking Cassie's hair. Maria held Cassie's hand the whole time.

"When does your mother get home?"

"Not until six."

"Can you telephone?"

"I've never been able to get through."

"We've got to do something." Mrs. Garcia thought for a moment. Then freeing herself from Cassie, she motioned to Maria to take her place. "Wait here. I'll call Manuel from the neighbor's."

Maria's father was home within fifteen minutes. He too put his arm around Cassie as soon as he saw her. "Come," he said. "Into the truck. We need to get your mother."

Cassie wasn't sure she knew what he meant. "You know where she works?" she asked.

Mr. Garcia nodded. "In the shipyard. It's not far. We'll all go."

Cassie had never been in the truck. At first, as she had gotten to know Maria, she had been haunted by memories of the truck and her accident. In the two years she had been coming to the Garcia home, those memories had begun to fade. Cassie now passed the battered pickup without feeling a thing. But she had never been inside.

Barely thinking about the truck, she stepped up on the running board and into the front seat. All four of them squeezed in as Mr. Garcia started the motor. As they drove, Cassie wasn't sure where they were going, but Manuel seemed to know his way.

Before long, he pulled the truck into a large parking lot and stopped at a gate.

"What d'you want?" A young attendant came out of a small building by the gate.

"We're looking for Nellie Clay. It's an emergency."

"Yeah? What kind of emergency."

Mr. Garcia remained calm. Cassie thought he seemed used to being hassled. "A death in the war," he said softly. "Please let us go through."

The youth let them in at once. "That way." He nodded toward a building off to the left with his head. "They'll call her for you there."

Mr. Garcia drove the truck closer to an office building near a corner of the lot. They climbed out of the truck and went inside.

Cassie still felt stunned. Mercifully, she didn't have to do anything at all. Mrs. Garcia continued to hold her, while Mr. Garcia did everything else.

Right now he was talking quietly to the secretary in the office. She nodded and picked up the phone.

Within three minutes, Nellie was in the office. The secretary must not have told her the reason for the call, for she looked puzzled as she saw Cassie and the group. She moved quickly to her daughter, to make sure she was all right.

"Cassie. What's up?"

"Oh, Ma." Cassie buried her head in her mother's breast. She started to say something else, but broke off in a sob. As the rest of the group remained silent, all eyes on her, she tried again. "Pa's dead. Killed in Italy."

"Oh my God." Nellie's knees buckled, and she looked around for somewhere to sit. A couple of torn vinyl chairs were set against the wall, and she sank down.

"How do you know?"

"Telegram."

"Are you sure?"

Cassie nodded.

"It's not a mistake?"

"I don't think so. It had his name and number. He was killed in Rome."

78

"Oh, no." Nellie buried her head in her hands.

Now it was Cassie's turn to try to comfort her mother. She sat down next to her, and the two held one another without saying a word.

Later that evening, Cassie and her mother were home alone. The Garcias had insisted firmly that they come back to their house to have something to eat. Cassie had felt strange about having her mother there; Maria was her friend and her mother hadn't seen the Garcias except Maria since the episode in the hospital two and a half years before. But her mother needed someone to look after her for a while, and Cassie knew she couldn't do it herself. Until her mother's friend, Sadie, got home from work, Cassie felt grateful for the offer of someone else to take charge.

It had been awkward there at first. No one knew quite what to say. But when Mrs. Garcia put food on the table, things got better. Her mother took a drink when it was offered, and looked like she was slowly beginning to feel better.

Later Mr. Garcia had driven the two of them home. "Good night, Cassie, Nellie," he said as he saw them to the door. "I'll check in on you tomorrow."

Now Cassie sat drinking a cup of tea with her mother at the kitchen table. Her mother kept looking at the telegram, as if hoping it would say something else if she read it just one more time.

"What're you thinking, Ma?" Cassie felt more like talking now.

"I don't know." Nellie stared off into space. "Half the time I feel vacant. The other half I try to remember how Pa looked."

"Did you really think this was going to happen, Ma?"

"I don't know," she said again. "I guess you're always afraid something like this's going to happen, but you don't ever expect it really will.

"I feel bad, Ma."

Her mother looked up, a puzzled expression on her face. "Of course you do."

"No, I mean I feel bad 'cause of what happened before."

"What do you mean?"

Cassie wanted her mother to understand, but wasn't sure she grasped what she was trying to say. "I felt..." Cassie paused, then started again. "I felt funny about Pa before he left."

Nellie nodded. "I know."

"It's like I was angry at him a lot. Sometimes he'd be really nice, but then he'd yell at me, and I'd be angry again. I didn't want to be, but I was."

"I saw that."

"I know you did. I just never knew if Pa saw what was going on. I know he cared, but I still wanted him to make things OK."

"Oh, Cassie."

Cassie was crying quietly now.

"Oh, Cassie. I know what you mean, but that doesn't help now."

"It's funny, but I felt better when he went away. All that time sneaking out to see Miko, 'cause he didn't like her. I didn't have to do that anymore. But then I felt bad again." She stopped for a moment, then started up again. "It helped when he started to write to me. It really did. And I liked moving the pins on my map. I thought it was dumb when you made me put up the map, but then I got to like playing with it."

Her mother just nodded.

"But now it's all over, and I keep thinking like maybe he was still mad."

"I don't think so, Cass. He wasn't easy, I know. But deep down he wanted good things for you and me. I loved him. And I know you did."

"I know Ma. I know."

"Well, Cassie, it's you and me now, just like it's been."

"Oh, Ma." Cassie hugged her mother and rocked with her, like she had with Mrs. Garcia earlier in the day. She still felt confused, but it felt good to be held again. She closed her eyes and let herself drift off to sleep.

CHAPTER 12

Homecoming

Cassie was sitting in front of the sewing machine in Maria's kitchen. It was summer again, and she and Maria were together every day, sometimes at one house, sometimes at the other.

"How's this, Mrs. Garcia?" Cassie asked as she held up a short black skirt.

"Not bad, Cassie." Mrs. Garcia looked over Cassie's shoulder, then took the skirt and stretched it out on the table. "The waist looks good. But watch you make the hem even when you stitch it by hand."

"I'll get it right. You'll see."

"I know you will." Mrs. Garcia smiled.

Cassie liked working with Maria's mother. She was learning more and more from Mrs. Garcia and was now making a party skirt to wear when school started again next month. She and Maria were about to start high school, and there would be dances in the fall. In eighth grade last year, the girls had started looking more carefully at the boys, and she and Maria now spent a lot of their time talking about the nicer ones in their class. Cassie's favorite was Joel, but he seemed shy whenever she was around. When she had bumped into him at the candy store last week, he had given her a lollipop, then mumbled something about the first dance. Cassie wasn't sure if he was asking her or not. She hadn't said anything, but hoped he would. If not, there was a Sadie Hawkins dance in October, when the girls got to ask the boys.

Picking up the black thread, she did the first few stitches on the hem, then remembered she had to get home to help her mother cook. "Thanks, Mrs. Garcia," she said as she left. "See you tomorrow, Maria. I'll be over about nine."

❖ ❖ ❖

The newspaper headline the next morning was big and bold. "ATOMIC BOMB HITS JAPAN" appeared just below the masthead of the *Los Angeles Times*.

Cassie didn't usually read the paper, but Nellie had brought it home today and left it out for her to see. The headline made Cassie anxious to learn more. She had been following the progress of the war in radio accounts, particularly after her father had been killed. The war in Europe was over now, and only the fighting in the Pacific dragged on. President Roosevelt had died months before, and Harry Truman was in the White House. All kinds of things were happening these days.

Cassie focused on the newspaper headline. What was an atomic bomb, she wondered. Would it make the war end?

A smaller headline beneath the first gave more details: "Man's Most Destructive Force, One Equal to 2000 B-29 Loads, Blasts Nips."

"Nips," she thought. Not a very nice word. Then again, we were at war with the Japanese.

Glancing at the front page, Cassie saw five stories about the atomic bomb. On the second page, there were still more accounts. Cassie began to read but found herself getting confused. She was relieved when her mother came back from a trip to the store.

"What's an atomic bomb, Ma?"

"You know as much as I do, Cass."

"No, I mean it. I don't understand what makes it different."

"I don't know. But it seems like it's a whole lot bigger than any bombs they had before."

"This story says the bomb landed on Hiroshima. Where's Hiroshima, Ma?"

"Beats me. Off in Japan somewhere."

"I've heard the name before. I wonder if that's where Miko's grandparents lived." Cassie thought for a moment about the devastation the newspaper account described and felt a chill. If Miko's grandparents had been there, they were probably dead.

Nellie looked up. "Things are rough for the Japanese all over. It doesn't look like they can last much longer."

"Do you think the war's going to be over soon?"

"I hope so. I'm tired of the war. I'm ready for a rest."

"Do you miss Pa?"

"I do. Even more now, I guess. And I don't suppose I'll really feel like it's all over and done with him 'til the fighting's stopped."

"It's funny. I felt more impatient before, when we couldn't get all the meat or sugar we wanted. But I guess I got used to it. And somehow, when Pa got killed, all that other stuff didn't seem to matter so much anymore."

"You're growing up, Cass. You're growing up."

Maria came over several days later after school.

"I heard on the news about another atomic bomb," Cassie said as they entered the door.

"Me too. My father says the war's just about over. He says the Japanese are going to have to give up."

"How does he know?"

"Reading the paper. Listening to the news."

"What's going to happen to your family when the war's over?"

"I don't know. What do you mean?"

"I reckon we're going to stay here in California," Cassie said. "You know, for a long time I thought we'd go back home to Tennessee. I really wanted to go at first, and I think my ma did too, only my pa wouldn't think of it. Now he's gone, but my ma's not eager to go back."

"Why not?"

"I guess she's afraid she couldn't work like she does up here. Jobs aren't as good. With Pa dead, she figures she's going to have to work, and she'd rather do it in California."

"We'll stay here, too," Maria said. "My father's hoping he can keep his job, or at least get something like it. Working in the factory's hard, but it's the best job he's ever had. I heard him and my mother talking the other day. We'll probably stay here in the project as long as we can. If they close it down, we'll look for somewhere else then."

Cassie looked out the window. "It's still not pretty," she said as she looked at the smokestacks in the distance. "But I guess it's not as bad as I once thought."

Maria smiled. "You get used to lots of things when you have to."

A few days later, as Cassie and her mother were eating dinner, she heard a knock at the door.

"Get it please, Cass."

"Who is it?"

"I don't know. Open up."

Cassie opened the door. Miko stood there on the porch.

"Hi, Cassie." Cassie just stared at her. Miko had a shy, tentative look on her face.

"Miko. You're home." Cassie wanted to run up and hug her, but something held her back. "Come in. Come say hello to Ma."

Miko looked inside. "Is it all right. I mean…."

Cassie understood. "It's OK. Don't worry. I'll tell you about it."

Miko followed Cassie back to the kitchen. Her mother stood up as the girls came into the room. "Miko. Welcome home." She went over to Miko and gave her a hug. "Sit down with us. Have a cup of tea. When did you get back?"

"Just yesterday. We'd been trying to leave for a while, but there were all kinds of forms. It took a long time."

"Are you back on the farm?"

Miko nodded.

"Is it all right?"

"Sort of. Someone moved in while we were gone. A lot of stuff's been stolen, and the place is a mess. But whoever was there's left, been gone a few months our neighbor says, and we can get back in."

"I guess you're lucky there. I've been reading how some people took over property and won't let it go."

Miko nodded again. "My father was real worried. He wrote to the neighbors near the end, and when he found the place was empty, he decided we'd come back and try to make it go again."

"I hope he can."

Miko looked around, still apprehensive. "Where's your father, Cassie?"

Cassie looked down. "Dead. He was killed last year in Italy."

"Oh, no."

Cassie knew she should say something more but didn't know what to say.

Her mother came to her rescue. "He was killed when the Army entered Rome. It's been a while, Miko. It's all right now."

Cassie felt all confused. She wanted to unburden herself about her father, but words wouldn't come. She wanted to ask Miko about the camp, but wasn't sure what to ask. She felt awkward having her mother there when she wanted to talk, but grateful for her presence since she wasn't sure what she wanted to say.

Her mother poured some tea, and the three of them sipped it silently for a few moments. Then her mother got up. "I'll clear the table and do the dishes tonight, Cass. You cooked. You can go with Miko."

Cassie felt a quick stab of fear. Why was she afraid, she wondered? Why couldn't she just open up?

"OK, Ma." She took a deep breath. "C'mon, Miko. Let's go outside."

On the porch Cassie paused, then sat down on the front stairs. Miko did the same.

She looked at the factory in the distance. "Nothing's changed," she said. "It all looks the same."

Cassie thought about that for a moment. "It may look the same, but it's not. I mean, the plant's still there, and the smokestack's still belching smoke. But it doesn't feel as bad as it used to."

"You can't believe how good this looks after where we've been."

Cassie was grateful for the opening. She wanted to find out about Miko's experiences. It also gave her a chance to think more about how to describe her own. "Was it really bad?"

Miko just stared out at the factory. "It was awful. All of it."

"Tell me about it," Cassie said softly.

"I was scared when we went," Miko said. "Packing everything up. My mother was crying. Being sent to the racetrack. Sleeping in an old horse stall. At least the family was together. But it was uncomfortable all the time. Kenshi was irritable. He and my father began to fight. Then, just as we were settling in, they moved us out to Utah."

"You wrote about that."

"It was worse than I described. The whole family was in one tiny room, in a ramshackle building, like hundreds of others."

Cassie looked down the street at other houses—all the same—in the project.

"Nothing like this at all. It made this look like paradise."

"Go on."

"We couldn't come or go as we pleased. We all had numbers. There was a fence around the whole place, and we felt like prisoners the whole time."

"How was your mother?"

"All right, except she hated the bathrooms. They weren't private at all—just a long row of seats—and she never really adjusted to that."

"I wouldn't either." Cassie smiled.

"It was no joke. And she was upset, too, that she couldn't cook. It was like all the things that she did that were important to her were gone."

"Did your father work?"

"After a while, in one of the shops they set up in the camp. He hated it, but it was something to do. But he got more moody all the time. He wanted to be back on the farm, and got real unhappy the longer we were away."

Cassie thought about her own father's restlessness, but this was different.

"What was worse," Miko continued, "was that he didn't feel like he was a father anymore. I mean, we knew he was and all, but he wasn't earning money and it made him angry. I heard him and my mother talk about that a lot at first. And then he just got quiet and didn't say anything anymore."

"Is he better now?"

"I hope so. He started to feel better when he found out the farm was free. We owned it and all, but he was afraid someone had just taken it. When he discovered it was empty, he began to think we could get back. And then he felt OK again."

"You wrote about a man getting killed when he was off by the fence."

"A sentry shot him dead. Called out to him, but the man was old and bending down and didn't hear. It was broad daylight, and he wasn't going anywhere, but the guard just fired and killed him."

"What happened then?"

"Nothing happened to the guard. The whole camp went to the funeral, and everybody got upset, but nothing much changed."

"Sounds spooky." Cassie paused for a few moments. Finally she spoke again. "I'm glad you're back."

"Me too. Your father, I guess he got drafted and sent overseas?"

Cassie nodded. "He went off to the Army, all excited about going off to Europe and seeing the world. And then he went and got himself killed."

"Oh, no." Miko waited a moment. "Was that bad for you?"

Cassie didn't answer. She just stared ahead.

"Is something wrong? I'm sorry if I asked something I shouldn't have."

"No, no. It's just that…." She paused, then didn't continue.

"You seem funny, Cassie. Far away."

"I…I don't know what's wrong."

"You know, all the time we were away, I dreamed of coming back, and of coming over here, and talking to you and telling you everything that went on. I guess I went over the scene hundreds of times in my mind. It kind of kept me going when it got all lonely there. But it doesn't feel right now. Somehow it's not the same."

"I'm sorry, Miko. I don't know what's wrong. I just…."

"I'm sorry, too, Cassie. Maybe it's my fault. Maybe I expected too much." A tear rolled down her cheek.

Cassie saw her begin to cry and felt even worse. She wanted to say something but still didn't know what to say. There was a distance there. Yet she had no idea what to do.

Cassie started to stand up, but Miko was on her feet first. She looked at Cassie with more tears welling up in her eyes, then turned and ran toward the street.

"Miko, come back."

Miko didn't turn but just kept running toward home.

CHAPTER 14

Reunion

Cassie and her mother sat eating breakfast at the kitchen table. It was Saturday, and her mother had the day off.

"What happened with Miko last night?"

"It was strange, Ma. It wasn't right."

"What do you mean?"

"I don't know. Miko was trying to be nice, and tell me what had happened to her. And somehow, I couldn't respond."

"Why not?"

"I told you. I don't know."

"Has she changed?"

"I'm not sure. She must have."

"Have you?"

Cassie just looked at her. "It's like...it's like I've felt funny for a long time. All the time she was writing me letters. I wrote back sometimes, but not always. I just didn't know what to say. But I always felt bad about not writing more."

"Is that all?"

Cassie looked down at her bowl of oatmeal. "No. I guess I felt funny about her, too 'cause of the war and fighting the Japanese."

"Oh, Cassie."

"I know I shouldn't have. But especially after Pa died I felt it. I know he was killed in Europe, but it was like it was all the same war. And without thinking too much about it, I guess I got angry at everybody we were fighting."

"But we weren't fighting Miko or the Yashimotos." Nellie's voice was gentle as she spoke.

"I know. And that's why I felt even worse for thinking that way."

"Cassie, Cassie, Cassie. Why didn't you say something?"

"You were busy, or away working. I had Maria and didn't have to think about Miko a lot. It was easy to forget about except when I got reminded by a letter or something."

"I haven't been away all the time."

"I know. I'm not blaming you."

"Anyway, I'm not going to be away so much for a while."

Cassie looked up. "Why not?"

"With the war just about over, Mr. Hardin, my boss in the shipyard, told us yesterday that most of the riveting and drill press jobs were going back to the men when they came home from the war."

"Oh, Ma. You wanted to keep working."

"I will. Got to, with your pa dead. I just don't know where."

"I'm sorry, Ma."

"It's not your fault. And anyhow, I didn't mean to change the subject. We were talking about you."

"I don't know what else to say."

"It was hard last night?"

Cassie nodded. "It was weird. Miko was acting like she had thought a lot about me when she was away and needed me, and I just couldn't help."

"Can you help now?"

"I don't know."

There was a knock at the door.

"That's not Miko again, is it?"

Cassie shook her head. "Should be Maria. She was coming over today."

Cassie went to the front door to let Maria in.

"Hello, Mrs. Clay, Cassie. You're still eating breakfast?"

Cassie looked at the table. "No, we're done. We just haven't cleaned up yet. We were just talking."

"I'm not interrupting anything?"

"No. We're done. Miko and her family are back. We were talking about that."

Maria frowned slightly. "Are they all right?"

Cassie started to answer, but her mother spoke first. "It sounds like they're OK," she said. "But I'm not so sure about Cassie. Maybe you can help her, Maria."

After dishes were cleared, Cassie and Maria were left alone.

"Let's walk over by the field," Cassie said. "I need to get out and do something."

Maria followed Cassie out the door. They headed toward the boundary of the project, and off into the field that used to remind Cassie of home. The dry grass still felt good as it brushed against her bare legs, but the memories of Tennessee were dimmer. Now she just enjoyed the sensation alone.

After walking in silence for a while, Maria spoke first. "What did your mother mean about you needing help?"

Cassie knew Maria would ask this and she had hoped she would, too. She took a deep breath. "It was really strange last night. Miko came over, and it was as if she needed to talk, but I couldn't say a word."

"Why not?"

"That's what I was talking to my ma about. It was like she hadn't changed much, but I had. I didn't know what to say. It used to be she was my best friend, but that was a long time ago. Now it felt different to me."

Maria walked along without answering. She reached down and pulled a long weed away from her toes.

"It made me feel all funny inside," Cassie went on.

"I feel like it's a little my fault."

"What d'you mean."

"Because I'm here, you don't feel as free to be friends with Miko again. Is that it?"

Cassie's brow creased as she thought about that for a moment. "Maybe. I wasn't thinking about it like that. I guess I've been talking with you all the time, like I used to with her before she went away. And now I don't know what to do." After a moment of silence, she looked over at Maria. "Are you jealous she's back?"

Maria tugged at a blade of grass and put it to her lips.

"No," she said at last. "I don't know Miko well. She was always nice to me in school. No, that doesn't bother me at all."

"You still look troubled."

"You've made a difference to me, Cassie. Knowing you has made me part of what's going on here. At school. With the other girls. Sometimes with the boys. It used to sound to me like you and Miko had something like this before, and I guess I was jealous then. But I'm not now. She needs you too, but there's room for me and her both."

"What should I do now?"

"I don't know."

"No, really. What can I do?"

"Maybe you should go over to her house and really try to talk. Like you didn't let yourself last night."

"Will you come with me?"

"Why should I?"

"It'd make it easier for me."

"It'd make it harder for her."

"Maybe. But I need you to come."

Maria thought about that for a few moments. "All right," she said at last. "I'll come."

Cassie felt her heart pounding as she knocked on Miko's door.

"Why, Cassie. Welcome back."

"Hi, Mrs. Yashimoto. But you're the one who's back."

"I suppose so. Who's this, Cassie. We haven't met."

"I'm sorry. This is Maria Garcia, Mrs. Yashimoto. She was in Miko's and my class at school before…."

Just then Miko appeared at the door. "Cassie!" She looked around and saw Maria without really recognizing her.

"This is Maria, Miko. You remember her, from Miss Daniel's class. A long time ago."

Miko nodded. "I remember. Valentines."

Maria smiled. "That was a while back. You do remember."

Mrs. Yashimoto looked at Cassie and smiled. "It's good to see you again. I want to find out how you've been, but I'll leave you girls alone for now. First though, Miko told me your father was killed in the war, Cassie. I'm sorry."

"Thank you," Cassie said. She paused for a moment. Should she ask, or shouldn't she, she wondered. This was as good a time as any, she decided. "Did your family come from Hiroshima?"

Mrs. Yashimoto shook her head. "Nagasaki," she said. "But that was just as bad. An atomic bomb landed there, too."

"Were they all right?" Cassie asked.

"We haven't heard yet," she answered. Her eyes narrowed, and she turned and left the room.

"I shouldn't have said anything," Cassie said softly.

"It's all right," Miko said. "It's all right." She looked at Cassie, then at Maria. "I'm glad you came over," she said finally. "I wasn't sure what would happen after last night."

"I'm sorry about that. I just felt all funny, and couldn't say anything at all."

"I guess I'd been dreaming about talking to you for so long that I had a picture in my mind of how I wanted things to be. It doesn't always work out that way." She glanced over at Maria. "Things change."

Maria saw Miko's glance, and looked down at the ground. Cassie wished she would say something, but Maria remained silent. "They don't change that much, Miko," Cassie said. "It's going to be OK."

"I don't want to intrude." Miko looked at Maria again.

"You're not."

"I hope not."

"And anyway, you're being silly."

"I'm sorry. I didn't feel silly last night."

"That was my fault."

There was an awkward pause. No one said a word. Cassie could feel the tension in the room.

Cassie's mind drifted back to the events of the past four years. Memories swirled around, like the wisps of smoke coming from the chimneys of the factories nearby. She thought of what each one of them had been through—of Miko being driven from her home, of Maria coming to California and feeling left out, of her own uprooting as she followed her father who saw the war as the key to his dreams but ended up dead.

Cassie caught herself, and came back to the present. For a moment she felt she was either going to laugh or cry. Without being able to control herself, she giggled, then took hold. "I'm sorry. I'm not trying to make light of this. But here we are like a bunch of little old ladies."

Miko remained stiff, her face tight. Maria, still silent, looked over at Cassie, and gave an almost imperceptible nod. Cassie knew what she meant.

"Miko."

Miko looked up.

"Miko, everything's changed, and nothing's changed. I want to find out all about your war and tell you about mine. Maria's had a hard time, too, and she helped me after you left. But you're back now, and I'm back, and it's all going to be all right."

"You're sure?"

Cassie nodded.

Miko gave an involuntary sob as if struggling to hold back tears.

Cassie knew what she had to do, what she should have done last night. She went over to Miko, put her arms around her and held her tight. "We love you, Miko," she said softly. "We do love you. And everything's going to be all right."